A DRAGON'S TREASURE

Beverly Ovalle

Paranormal Romance

Paranormal Romance

A Dragon's Treasure
Copyright © 2017 Beverly Ovalle
ISBN: 0996797378

ISBN 13: 978-0996797375
First E-book Publication: June 2017
First Print Publication: June 2017

Cover design by Jo-Anna Walker
Edited by Magic Wand Editing
All cover art and logo copyright © 2017 by Beverly Ovalle

PUBLISHER
Midwest Dragon Press

Dedication

To the ladies at Higher Grounds Coffee Shop! You let me hide so I can write. You only had to chase me out a couple of times so you could close. I'll be back just to enjoy the coffee alone!

To my beta readers, you have seen this before it became the book it is now. What a transformation! I couldn't have done it without you.

To my family. I love you all. Thank you for your support!

• CONTENTS

A DRAGON'S TREASURE

Beverly Ovalle

Paranormal Romance

CHAPTER ONE

A dragon's most desired treasure is his mate. After all his centuries, he still waited for his. Kai drooped, exhaling, stirring the treasures he'd collected around him. The musical tinkle of the shifting coins beneath him echoing throughout the chamber. Echoing like the empty place in his heart. He sighed. His nose wrinkling when just a hint of smoke came with it.

Kai established his lair in this rich and verdant land that called to his soul. Rich in coal and gold, it called to his dragon, enticing him. Kai rumbled, his gut churning. He shot out flames, relieving the ache in his stomach. They licked the walls, adding to the shine. Over the centuries his flames formed the walls surrounding his hoard into diamonds. It didn't stop the longing in his soul.

Kai scratched at the gold beneath him, his claws digging in. Tension filled him. Normally, burrowing into his gold helped. Today? Not so much.

He needed his mate. Alone for longer than he cared to think about, he ached to find her, love her. He knew she would come here. He didn't know how or why, but Kai was sure of this. He believed it with his whole heart and soul.

Once shifters came out, Kai traveled extensively, a necessity to move on or be killed. Those days were long past and the need to constantly flee abated.

Dragons were eyed warily when they finally stepped out of the realms of legend. The last group of shifters to make themselves known to man. Too many shifters were exterminated when they disclosed their existence. Dragons lived too long not be wary of man. Unlike most shifters, rumors of dragons existed since man began to talk. Little did humans realize dragons walked among them.

Kai's heart ached. He'd lost his parents more than two centuries past to superstition and hate. Bounties on the lives of dragons, sent fool-hardy hunters after his parents. His mother caught unaware, pierced through the heart by a crossbow.

His father went berserk at her death. His revenge against the hunters bloody.

Kai burrowed deeper into his pile, flames flickering from his snout.

His father, hunted for bounty by the same people who murdered his mother, was shown no mercy. Caught, drawn and quartered, his head hacked from his body, and paraded around the village on a pike.

He breathed deeply, releasing a stream of steam that rose from between the coins. He ground his teeth, remembering. His talons clenched fistfuls of gold, squeezing, seeking relief. Seeking calm, even after all this time. No matter how much time passed, he missed them.

Kai and his siblings eradicated the village. He rumbled, eyes gleaming. The satisfaction of seeing his parent's murderers plead for mercy a balm to his soul. Blood flowed, their bodies torn apart. Kai swallowed, the metallic taste of their blood, one he wouldn't forget. The repercussions tore the siblings apart. Forced to flee and separate to save themselves, Kai rarely saw them since.

The lessons of his past too fresh in his mind, Kai stirred, sending more gold tumbling. Some humans believed they were too dangerous to live. He snorted. They always had, and some always would. The hate groups lessened, but still existed. Murder of a shifter finally became a hate crime and punishable by law.

Kai growled. Nothing stopped it completely, but it was at least safe for the most part now. Dragon hunters few and far between.

Myth whispered, to a dragon there were two categories of life forms, no matter the species, prey or mate. Even other shifters gave them a wide berth because of this. Kai chuckled. They were smarter than he usually gave them credit for. The shorter life spans of humans and other species aided their acceptance. What once was fact was now considered fantasy, and dragons preferred it that way. One of the reasons Kai rarely revealed his true self to humans.

Kai rumbled, the memories continuing. Able to move among dragons and men, dragon shifters lived the best of both worlds. Taking human form, Kai had been a Mate Hunter. He searched for his mate and while doing so, identified others. An honored job among dragons. He preened. He was one of the best.

In the early days, those marked as dragon's mates were set up as sacrifices. Integrating into the human populous easy enough, Kai identified the mates in his human form, setting them up for sacrifice. Once they were tied up and left alone, he changed and carried them away as a dragon, usually with the superstitious villagers' blessings. They never knew the man picking out the sacrifices and the dragon were one and the same.

Kai chuckled. If the villagers only knew he took them away to a better life, they would have scrambled to be chosen. They would rather sacrifice a fellow human than have a Dragon terrorize the village, an outcome he made sure they thought would happen. A few well-timed fly-bys, a scattering of flocks and a few bursts of fire enough to convince them. Not to mention a quick meal.

Kai licked his chops. He had a fondness for mutton. He took full advantage of their superstition and fear. Kai rumbled, nostalgic, he sure missed those days.

Kai took those marked as dragon's mates and brought them to a dragon strong hold. Marked by birth, these men and women were pampered, adored, and protected by their mates. But that was long ago, man became more sophisticated, and dragons became fewer. They became legends and the old ways died.

Kai blew out a breath of air and stretched. His mind circling back, once again, to his need, his desire. Too long alone, he needed his mate. Ached to be bound to another's happiness. He believed somewhere, somehow, he would find his mate. His heart twisted. He couldn't be destined to be alone.

Kai glanced around, admiring his lair. He'd leave and then come back for a while, staying a bit longer each time, adding to his hoard. He didn't know what it was that kept calling to him. Finally, he gave into the pull. He stayed. Something inside of him settled down. Yearned, still, but settled back, waiting. He was so tired of waiting.

Long before humans discovered the rich veins of

coal in the area, Kai established his lair. He saw the fresh untouched land, smelled the hint of gold below. A thrill ran through him. This land, his land, hid many treasures the humans didn't find then, still hadn't found. They were his now.

Kai searched, finding an opening of a cave. Following the scent of gold, he established his lair. He settled there, mingling with the closest town, establishing his right to the land.

It felt right, instinctive to establish it here. Mining and lumber were the major industries in the county, the rape of the land below and above a typical human occupation. He shook his head, stretching. They destroyed anything they could get their hands on. His land, rich in coal deposits, lead deep into undiscovered caverns. The spring originating near his lair, swirling down through the rocky ground and creating a waterfall and pool in his cavern, also fed and formed the stream leading to the lake at the center of town miles away. The farming community grew up around it, covering the scarring left behind as the timber industry moved further away.

Kai looked around his lair, nosed a bit of his treasure to a more comfortable position, admired it, and settled again. The cool depth of the cavern, the treasure surrounding him, set him at ease, seeping deep into his bones. He prepared his lair, waiting for his mate. Coal once lined the walls down here, now it was refined. Year after year he breathed his fire, changing the once dirty and dusty coal into diamonds, another treasure he guarded carefully. Expanding the caverns found the gold he sensed, a singular talent of his. The indirect sunlight filtering through the caves, glittered as it bounced from diamond to diamond lighting up his cavern and shining on the deposits of gold interspersed amongst them. Kai wiggled joyfully, his treasure room truly a treasure. His mate would love it.

The town grew and Kai didn't spend as much time in his lair as he liked. Today, however, he needed to come here. His emotions pinging back and forth made a trip here imperative. Just entering centered him. Most forgot, perhaps never even knew, that this land belonged to him. He liked it that way, preferring the privacy.

He farmed, raising crops and cattle to be able to

keep his homestead in the early years. Kai absorbed more land until his dragon thrummed with satisfaction. He refused to sell to the logging companies. His land was rich in trees and natural prairies. He continued to blend in with the human population. Easily able to survive when all but the hardiest of humans didn't.

Work, rather than money, was how land was deeded when this country began. Afterward, he 'inherited' it through the years to keep the humans from turning against him and hide the fact he aged slowly. Until the dragons finally came out and he could be himself.

Kai preserved the original homestead. Centered in the mass of land he owned, an anchor to the past. He kept it in the best shape possible. Nothing of value a dragon owned was ever cast aside. He appreciated many things from the past. Craftsmanship never lost value. Hand carved furniture decorated his home. Kai himself created the door knobs from the diamonds in his lair. He worked precious gems into the stained glass windows. They worked in the décor in a way no one would know their value. The few privileged to visit assumed they were colored glass. But, he knew. He loved standing in the front room, the colors bursting across him in the rays of the sun. A piece of his hoard nearby kept his dragon happy, until recently.

Kai couldn't explain the urgency beating in his heart. The last week everyone tiptoed around him at work. More than once he'd snapped out orders, frustration twisting his gut. The reason he sought out the direct comfort of his hoard. His chest tightened, his heart beating faster than normal. A sharp exhilaration, an almost rabid excitement thrumming through his veins made the trip necessary. Kai needed to be here, his treasure surrounding him, calming him. His life was about to take a turn. For better or worse he didn't know, but he was old enough to be able to handle whatever came his way.

The tinkle of coins, shifting beneath his weight soothed him. The sparkle of sun bouncing on his treasure, glittering off his diamond walls calmed the pacing beast. The urgency abated, Kai knew it was time to head back to town. He sighed, wiggled down one more time into his hoard, wallowing in his gold, and then reluctantly rose.

Time to go.

Kai scrabbled off his pile of gold, slipping and sliding until firm ground met his claws. Shifting, he put his work clothes back on. He smirked, no need to come up out of his hoard and be noticed. Pulling on his jeans and plaid button up, Kai got ready to head back to work. He worked on the farm next to his land. He'd been doing it for years. He ran his spread and it was easy enough to help out his neighbors, occasionally. Or it was. Now, it was more like a full-time job.

Shaking his head, he snorted. The current owner recently mated a werewolf and didn't have a clue how to run the place. Casey, the former owner asked him to stay on and help her. Ellen begged him to help, too. He'd known her as a babe and couldn't say no. So, he'd temporarily moved into the foreman's house. His goal was to get her mate Breccan and his brother Max up to speed and then hand it over to them. Kai would be around for questions, but wolves and dragons didn't necessarily make the best of packs.

Stretching, then dropping into a chair that should have been in a throne room, and in fact once reigned in one. Kai put his socks and boots on. He slid his fingers along the smoothly polished arm. Every bit of his hoard held memories, some good, some not so much, but every bit imbued with memories that made up his life.

He would be glad when he could turn over the farm to Ellen. Where there were two wolves, there would soon be more. If they got him mad, he'd have no problem having a little crunchy wolf barbeque. Kai wouldn't be able to help himself. That would be the end of a peaceful existence.

Lone wolves didn't last long without a pack. Since Breccan mated Ellen, he was no longer in danger of being put down as a lone wolf. There was a story there, but Kai wasn't interested enough to pry. They were just wolves, after all. They weren't dragons.

****

"Why am I in this God forsaken town?" Connie mumbled. She needed to get out of Chicago and visiting her cousin in the back of beyond in Wisconsin, seemed like a good idea at the time. Knowing the small town would be a good place to hide out from the man trying to kill her clinched it. But the heat! She couldn't remember it ever being this hot. She regretted bringing the convertible since it had no air conditioning.

She'd folded the top down to catch a breeze. It didn't help. The air smothered her, wrapping her in a blanket of heat and humidity. The air itself hazy. She stopped at a traffic light, spying a man standing and waiting to cross. Connie's mouth dried. She couldn't help but stare. He was mopping his neck with his shirt and muscles rippled in his arms and abdomen. Yummy! Abs to die for, a bit of chest hair with a mouthwatering glory trail running down into low slung Levi's. A shiver ran through her body. Maybe this trip wouldn't be so bad if eye candy like this was around.

A slight breeze swirled in the air, fluttering her hair. The breeze continued to waft past the man. It wrapped around him, and his eyes snapped to hers. He lifted his head in the air and sniffed. If she didn't know better, she'd swear he could smell her. The weight of his gaze, the sudden stillness in his body made her catch her breath. The intent in his eyes, the feel of being his prey froze her. The light turned green. Unnerved, she turned away and drove off, just knowing his eyes followed her.

Connie shook her head driving to the edge of town. Trying to laugh away her paranoia. Prey indeed! She didn't know why the weight of his gaze flustered her, but she wasn't about to worry about it. Her life was complicated enough at the moment.

Her GPS told her to turn right, but there was no road. Dammit! Why did her cousin have to move out of town? Connie re-inputted Ellen's address into the destination.

"Calculating."

Connie eyed the GPS, cursing under her breath. She should have used the GPS on her cell phone, but wanted to make sure it was fully charged if she needed it. So, she used the beast her parents swore by, or swore at, depending on who was doing the talking. She should have known better.

Okay, there it was. Connie groaned. She had to make a U-turn; she missed the turn. Connie checked for traffic, *yeah right*, she rolled her eyes and turned the car around. Luckily, the car had a tight turn radius keeping her out of the ditch. Peering out the window she laughed to herself. If it didn't she would've called AAA to be towed.

Back on track, Connie hummed to herself. No matter why she left Chicago, she was excited to see Ellen. Living just blocks from each other as they grew up, they were more like sisters than cousins. When Connie and her family moved away in the beginning of their sophomore year, they were still able to drive to see each other. The next year, Connie's dad got another promotion and they moved to Chicago. Her parents wouldn't let her drive the many miles by herself. Once they started college, they were too busy to see each other more than a couple times a year.

She hadn't heard from Ellen since she bought the farm. Connie snorted. She still thought Ellen was nuts. The only one ever kicked out of FFA, owning a farm!

Connie laughed at the memory. 'But the cow was lonely' Ellen said. Leave it to Ellen to put the bull in the pen with the milk cows! Farmer Barrows was pissed, he lost half of his dairy herd when they turned up expecting. How a small town country girl could be so stupid about animals absolutely amazed her.

She sure did miss Ellen, though. The last time they'd partied together they celebrated their twenty-first birthdays. Only a month a part in age, they did everything together. Getting together for such a momentous age, a no brainer. Ellen met her in Chicago and they took the Metra further into the city to party. Two days later, a call to Connie's brother to pick them up, and they were puking in Connie's dorm room feeling like they'd died.

Connie's chest tightened. Shortly after, Ellen had been assaulted. Life changed overnight. Connie came up almost every weekend, but nothing helped. Lots of tears and hugs later, Ellen finally agreed to therapy. The next thing Connie knew, Ellen bought a farm and moved outside of town, deeper into Wisconsin.

The catalyst, the hellhounds following Ellen home. Aunt Maggie said they seemed to help and Connie agreed. Scary and looking way too much like wolves for Connie's peace of mind, they were definitely protective. Something Ellen needed.

Ellen gained some of the confidence she lost, her

eyes losing some of the fear in them. Ellen talked to them like they were people. Insisting they were shifters. Connie shook her head. If it made Ellen feel better, she wasn't arguing with her. She'd just told Ellen not to go around telling people that, they would think she was crazy. Connie did wonder though. They were almost too big to be natural.

She hadn't been to visit Ellen since she'd moved to the farm, but talked to her on the phone. Ellen was doing better, Connie could tell by her voice. The calls gradually went back to their normal routine, whenever one had a problem they would call or visit. Probably three to four months passed since they'd last talked. Texts didn't really count, usually just a 'How u doing? Miss U or LOL!'

Now, here they were, Ellen on a farm because of her massive dogs, and Connie in hiding from a maniac because she witnessed a drug deal gone wrong. She admitted, the thought of Ellen's dogs there made Connie feel safer too.

She shook her head, hands tightening on the wheel. God, if she hadn't been so upset at what she'd seen, she wouldn't have driven to Matt's. She always called her oldest brother with a problem no matter how stuffy he could get. It was instinctive to turn to him. Problem was, his blood was blue through and through and he made her report it. Then the screw up at the line up and the perp's buddy saw her. She still wasn't sure if it was deliberate or not. She knew the Chicago PD did everything they could to clean up their reputation over the years, but there would always be corrupt cops, and Chicago seemed to attract more than their fair share.

Connie shuddered. The man followed her to her apartment building! Thank God it was a secured building. But she still didn't feel safe with them knowing where she lived. She called Matt and told him she was going into hiding, told him about being followed. She gathered up as many clothes as she could, packing hurriedly as she talked. Hanging up with Matt cursing the situation and vowing to contact Internal Affairs, she grabbed her bags and left out the back exit of the parking garage, using her parent's convertible.

Thank goodness the exit was on the opposite side of the block and her parents out of town. Living in the building her parents owned had some perks, but she always ended up taking care of their place when they were gone. Normally, she'd bitch up a storm, but in this instance, she thanked her lucky stars.

She had asked Matt to contact Brookfield Zoo and explain what was happening. Working as an intern at Brookfield when all this went down, she doubted she'd be offered an internship there again. Maybe when she got to Ellen's she could work with a veterinarian in town so it wouldn't be a total loss.

Her mind raced. Connie wasn't sure how she even remembered to think about her internship. Panic spurring her decisions. She needed to go. Thinking of her job helped ease the shaking, brought her mind back to getting out, and finding a place to hide.

Connie made another turn and rolled her eyes. 'Turn right on County Road DE. You'll be on this road for a while.' Say what? This GPS was pathetic. Well, at least it was directing her to Ellen's place, hopefully. She followed the directions and it brought her to a mailbox with Ellen's name. Connie sat up straighter. Finally! This trip took her four hours give or take. She glanced at the gas gage. Thank goodness her parents always made sure they filled their tank to the brim. In her rush, she didn't even checked the gauge, just the mirror to make sure she wasn't followed.

Connie pulled up in the drive and parked near the house. She took a deep breath, exhaling shakily. She'd made it. Another breath pulled in the fresh country air. Connie relaxed, excitement creeping in. Too long since she'd seen her cousin. Glancing around, she didn't see Ellen anywhere outside. Connie hoped she was home. The only movement she saw were the animals standing lazily in their pens, tails twitching in the sultry air. Connie pulled her phone out and dialed.

"Hello," Ellen answered.

"Hey cuz! Whatcha doing?" Connie stifled her giggle. Wouldn't Ellen be surprised to see her? Regardless of why she was here, Connie couldn't wait to see her cousin.

"Starting dinner." She heard Ellen giggle and murmurs in the background.

"Got enough for one more?"

"What?" Ellen screeched. "Where are you?"

"Sitting in your driveway." Connie heard the phone drop, and got out of the car. She slipped her phone in her purse and leaned against the car door. She didn't have long to wait.

Ellen came barreling out of the door and grabbed Connie in a huge hug. They stood there, arms wrapped around each other absorbing the reassuring warmth of each other's body.

Connie squeezed tighter, eyes hot behind her closed lids. "God, I've missed you."

"Me too." Ellen's voice was muffled, buried in Connie's hair.

A throat cleared behind Ellen.

Connie looked up, eyes widening. "Wow. Who's this Ellen?"

The girls stepped apart. Ellen reached and grabbed the hand of the man behind her. Connie thought, *Green eyes and black hair, yum!* "Holy cow, Ellen, where have you been hiding him?"

"In the barn." A deep rumble from behind Connie caused her to whip around.

"I've died and gone to heaven. Ellen, wow, just

wow." Ellen was laughing and the men sported grins on their faces. "I take it this one is free?" She arched an eyebrow at Ellen.

"No." Ellen wore a smirk on her face. "Sorry cuz, he's unavailable."

Connie looked at the hand Ellen was holding and back to the blue eyed dark haired hottie behind her. "Spill it! What on earth have you been getting up to out here?"

Ellen's eyes sparkled. "I'm so happy! I'd like you to meet Breccan and his brother Max. But come on, grab your bag. You are staying, right? Dinner is almost done and I'll tell you everything that's been happening."

Connie glanced back. Cute, but he didn't stir any feelings in her. Not like the hottie on the street corner. "What exactly does unavailable mean? Is he married? Got a girlfriend?" She waggled her brows. "You enjoying both of them? Greedy girl."

"No." Ellen snickered. "Breccan doesn't share."

"Then he's available."

"Not according to him."

"Oh God, he's gay. What a waste."

Connie turned at a growl, Max scowling down at

her.

Ellen snorted. "He's not gay."

"If you say so." Connie giggled. The look on Max's face assured her he wasn't. She couldn't resist teasing him though.

"I'm not gay." Max's words came out in a growl.

Ellen and Connie snickered. The scowl on his face making her heart lighter. Sue her, she was a bit perverse.

"Come on, let's get dinner on the table before it burns. And Max eats you." Ellen linked arms and turned toward the house.

"Only if it's in a fun way." The growl behind her got louder. "You're positive he's not gay?" Connie said it in a stage whisper, unable to resist.

Ellen laughed, pulling her away. "You're still a trouble maker! You can stay in the guest room. You are staying, aren't you?"

"If you don't mind." Connie could feel his stare boring into her back. "They won't mind?" The door slammed shut behind them. Connie sniffed at the smells coming from the stove. Her stomach growled.

"He'll get over it." Ellen smirked. "It'll do him

good to get teased. He's too serious. I'd love to have you stay as long as you want. Here you go." Ellen waved toward a door inside the room. "It even has its own bathroom."

"Awesome." Connie dropped her bags and gave Ellen a hug. "It's so good to see you. I can't wait to spend time with you." She giggled. "And tease his hotness."

"I can't wait." Ellen squeezed her again, then stepped back. "Come on, I have to get supper off the stove."

"I could eat." Connie followed Ellen out, her shoulders relaxing. "It smells so good." She could breathe, finally. She'd been tense since she witnessed that poor man die. She shuddered. Connie didn't think she'd ever forget the sight of his blood exploding from his head.

"Well, let's do it then."

Dinner was fantastic. Connie and Ellen chatted about growing up together. Breccan laughing with them and Max glaring at her. Connie couldn't help but flirt with Max, the more she did the harder he frowned.

Connie and Ellen looked at each other and laughed.

"Lighten up, bro. I think they have your number." Breccan smirked, bumping Max's arm.

"Whatever." Max rolled his eyes, but Connie was glad to see his expression lighten.

Connie stood, and loaded the dishwasher while Ellen put on a pot of coffee then headed into the living room. Connie flopped onto the loveseat and Ellen the couch. Breccan sat and pulled Ellen into his arms. Max leaned against the doorway, an empty coffee cup in his hand.

Ellen shooed the men away. "I want to talk girl talk. Go to bed, or hang out in the barn, okay? Can you put Connie's car in the garage first?"

"Sure." Breccan stood up.

"My keys are on the counter." Connie added.

Breccan pulled Ellen into a kiss. "We'll be in the barn for a bit." When Breccan released her, Ellen was breathless. The men left through the kitchen and they could hear one of them grabbing the car keys.

Connie was fanning herself. "Wow!" Connie couldn't stand it any longer. "Holy cow, Ellen! Where did you meet them?"

Ellen laughed.

"Remember my hellhounds, as you called them? They're wolves. The ones that followed me home. You didn't believe me, no one did, that they were shifters."

"I can't believe you were right! That is so awesome, that they're really shifters! Talk about hot!"

"Oh, yeah and I'm Breccan's mate." She sighed, a wide smile on her face. "I've never been so happy."

"I'll bet." Connie laughed, pleased as punch for her cousin. "I'm so glad Ellen." She gave her a hug, tears in her eyes. "I'm so glad." Connie sat back and eyed Ellen. "So, how did you find out they were shifters?"

Ellen's face turned pink and she giggled.

"Breccan, err, changed when we were playing in the barn."

"This I have to hear! Dish."

"No way, I'm not going to kiss and tell."

"Spoilsport."

They giggled and joked around and caught up on their lives. Mostly it was about Ellen's life. Connie wasn't sure how to tell Ellen what she saw or even if she should. Her stomach twisted. She'd keep it quiet for now. Hopefully, she'd be safe here. Maybe she wouldn't even have to mention what happened. Connie yawned, her jaw cracking.

"Time for bed before the sun comes up." Ellen stood and stretched. The men came back in a while ago, poking their heads in to see that they were still up before heading to bed.

"Sounds good to me." Connie's body ached from the long drive. Another yawn and her ears popped. "I'll see you in the morning."

CHAPTER TWO

Kai's eyes followed the flashy convertible. He breathed in the scent drifting on the breeze. Her scent, spicy and fresh clenched his gut, snagging his attention. He stared, eyes following her until she was a speck in the distance. Finally crossing when she was out of sight. He didn't recall seeing her before. He was intrigued enough to wonder if he would run across her again.

Kai was heading to the dealership to pick up a truck he'd dropped off earlier. He slid a hand in his pocket. The feel of the gold nugget centered him. No dragon could be without a bit of treasure. He'd dropped the truck off and ate lunch with Casey, the old man who'd sold his farm to Ellen.

The truck had been having brake problems and his boss, Ellen, wanted it fixed. She planned on taking it herself until Breccan put his foot down. It was fine for Kai to risk driving it, but not Ellen. The werewolf guarded his mate jealously. Kai knew he would wrap her in plastic and hide her away from everything if he could. His chest ached. Kai would do the same when he found his. If he ever found his. Mates were precious to all shifters.

Coming into town, Kai enjoyed catching up with Casey. He was a likeable old guy and selling the farm hit him hard. Kai kept him updated on crops and the breeding program, made him feel like he was still involved. Ellen knew Casey her whole life, so she didn't mind. On occasion Kai would find her on the phone with the old man asking advice.

He pushed the door of the dealership open, and the air conditioning swept over him. The chill felt good after the heat outside. Kai slid his arms into his shirt leaving it unbuttoned. He headed to the service counter. "Hey Jim, truck done yet?"

"Yup. It had a split in the brake line. Pads and

rotors were still good. We checked out the master cylinder too. It passed with flying colors. You're due for an oil change in about another thousand miles and we filled all the fluids up."

"Great. Thanks."

"So, what's on the agenda for the rest of the day?" Jim leaned against the counter.

"Just picking up the truck. Visited with Casey already. A low-key day. Run a few errands, hit the bar before I head back to the farm. We're getting pretty self-sufficient. I didn't think Ellen would take so well to being a farmer. Breccan is coming along too."

Jim snorted. "Ellen. If you could fail 4H that girl would. She tried hard, but she never seemed to get the hang of things. It was a big surprise when she bought old man Casey's farm."

"Well, she needed the room for her dogs." In a farming community Kai knew better than to refer to them as wolves. Regardless of the truth, in their natural form they scared people. Huge, even for wolves. They were just as big when they were human. Kai shook his head. It was a miracle Ellen didn't run screaming. Then again, it was people that scared her, with good reason.

"Hell hounds. I ain't never seen dogs that big. Ellen was almost run out of town! Everyone was scared of those things. Her dogs did more to keep the people following the leash laws than anything. Hardly any strays. People were afraid if their pets were loose those monsters would eat them." Jim laughed. "Craziest thing. Everyone was pretty glad they moved outside of town. Course now people aren't so careful of their pets. Had a couple of bites in the last few weeks. Now they're grumbling 'cause of that."

Kai grinned. "I could ask them to wander into town for a bit."

Jim snickered. "Keep everyone on their toes. So, are they really shifters?"

"Yeah, why?"

"Well, Ellen's one of us. Just want to make sure she's all right."

"Better than all right. Happiest I've ever seen her. Turns out she's Breccan's mate."

"Damn, I'd heard rumors. Hard to believe. So, they're really werewolves? That explains their size, I suppose." Jim shook his head. "So, when's the weddin'?"

"Mating is more permanent than a wedding."

"Not around here. Ellen ain't just another ho, you know. Her daddy'll be wantin' a weddin'. You wait and see." Jim nodded. "Hell, Ellen'll be wantin' one too. I'm surprised her elder or the pastor hasn't been over yet."

"Hmm…you're right. Well, I better warn Breccan. Ellen may assume a wedding will be coming, but I know it probably hasn't crossed his mind at all. I don't want to see her hurt or hear talk about her in town." Kai idly buttoned up his shirt. "He just wants her happy."

Jim snorted. "There's always talk in town. Gossip is a way of life out here, not much else to do. Well, you warn him, tell him our expectations. Ellen's a good girl." Jim put the truck keys on the counter. "Here ya go, trucks outside."

"Thanks, Jim." Kai grinned and grabbed the keys. "I'll mention the leash problem too."

Jim laughed as Kai left. "You do that."

Kai ran a few other errands and by the time he finished, night was at hand. His stomach rumbled. Time for dinner. The traffic noises died down and the diner's neon sign zapped in the quiet of the evening. Swinging open the door, Kai stepped in. The aroma of beef sent a gurgle twisting through his belly.

Barbie waved him to his usual seat. Weeknights tended to attract the bachelors in town. Kai sat, looking around. The few women there flirted with the grinning men. Kai often thought they ought to just label one night 'single's night' and the place would be packed with women and men.

"The usual?" Barbie set down a glass of water and clean silverware.

"Yes, please." The cook made a mean pot roast. It was the special for today. The full plates and home cooked taste the reason the single men flocked there. Kai sniffed, pulling the scent in. He held back a growl.

"Enjoy." Barbie returned, setting a full plate in front of him, and turned away.

It smelled great. His stomach protested, aching to be filled. Kai dove in, the beef melting on his tongue.

Shoveling the last bite of supper down, Kai sat back and groaned, his pants tight as usual after a meal here. He leaned back, taking a deep breath. Barbie made sure he always ate enough. It didn't hurt she knew to double his servings. A dragon needed to keep up his strength after all. Kai stood, dropping his money on the table.

"Thanks, Barbie. Delicious as always." He patted his stomach, waving as he left.

"Thanks, Kai. Have a good night." She waved, turning back to another customer.

Kai walked around the building to the parking lot. The humidity wrapped around him. The sound of crickets died, starting up again with each step past them. Climbing in, the truck started like a dream. Kai unbuttoned his waistband with a sigh. He pumped the brakes leaving the lot. He nodded, satisfied. The brakes were working correctly again.

Kai headed back to the farm, enjoying the peacefulness of the night. The sound of the tires on the asphalt, soothing. Ellen's farm was just far enough outside town that it seemed to be in its own little world. Kai enjoyed that. Dragons weren't really social creatures. He didn't mind people, but preferred to not be surrounded by them all of the time. He liked the fact his place was even farther away. He drummed his fingers against the wheel. He'd be able to concentrate on his own property alone, soon. Breccan and Max were quick studies. Hopefully, it wouldn't take them too long to learn the ins and outs of the farm. They'd been pretty secretive about their background, so Kai didn't know if they were familiar with working the land.

The peaceful night encouraged him to drive around. Even though not all the property in the area belonged to him, he'd watched it build up. Saw the families move in and grow. Kai drove, checking the farms settling down for the night. It settled his dragon. Territory to him didn't really match land deeds. As far as he was concerned, everything he'd watched grow belonged to him, people included. Kai smirked. It was a dragon thing.

Circling back to Ellen's farm Kai turned into the drive, the gravel crunched under the tires. It was late, and only a light in the main house shown bright.

Kai nodded, glancing around. On the surface Colin did a good job of settling everything for the night. Kai wondered how long he would stay. Colin was part of the local coyote pack. A bit unusual, one of them working another farm. Colin showed all the earmarks of being an alpha, so perhaps trouble with his alpha drove him out. If he was thinking of striking out on his own, it made sense for him to learn all he could. He'd been pretty closed mouthed about his motives. He was a hard worker and that was all Kai cared about.

Kai pulled the truck up to his cabin and got out. His nostrils caught an elusive scent. It brought to mind beaches and blue eyes. The image of the beauty he'd seen earlier flashing across his memory. There was no way she'd be here. Shrugging off the urge to investigate it further, Kai headed in and stripped, settling for the night. Morning would be soon enough to talk to Breccan and follow the scent wrapping around him.

The crows of the cockerel greeted the day. Stretching, Kai rolled out of bed. The heat in the small cabin stifling. Naked, he headed to the bathroom. Turning the water to cold, he stepped in. Kai shivered, enjoying the coolness. The cold water, woke him up further. The day promised to be hotter, based on the temperature already. Fire dragon or not, he didn't need heat all the time. The cold beads of water beating on his head, were welcome on his sweaty skin. Kai breathed deeply, standing under the spray. Finally, he soaped up and rinsed off. Stepping out, he shook. The air was so warm he didn't even need to towel off. Definitely another scorcher. Dragging on a pair of jeans, he headed out. Time to start his day.

Kai went through his morning routine, keeping an eye out for one of the wolves. He finished unhooking the dairy cows and got them settled when he spied Breccan. He was crunching on something, growling as Kai drew near. Damn dogs and their bones. Like he'd bother to steal its paltry meal. Kai ignored the warning growl. They both knew who would win in a fight. It wasn't the puppy dog.

Kai looked around. Early enough, Ellen probably wasn't up yet. She didn't need to hear this conversation. No telling what her reaction would be if she did. He cared enough about her to not want her to overhear. Breccan finished eating and looked up. Breccan narrowed his eyes and growled. Kai growled right back. He glared at Breccan. "Barn. Talk." He turned and went into the barn.

Breccan glared after him. His attitude said that no damn dragon was bossing him around. Kai wasn't surprised when he took his time following him into the barn. Wolves might be brave, but sometimes it bordered on stupidity. Luckily Kai had a soft spot for Ellen. A bit of wolf for a snack was a distinct possibility.

Breccan entered, and Kai turned to face him. "Shift, dog. I've a few questions for you."

Breccan looked at him, attitude in every line. He shifted. "What do you want?"

"I need to talk to you about Ellen."

"What about Ellen?" Breccan narrowed his eyes at Kai. "She is no concern of yours, she's my mate." He was growling by this time, eyes shifting in warning.

Kai growled back. Dumb ass dog, more courage than sense. "I know that. But that's why I need to talk to you." Kai stared, hard-faced as Breccan continued to give off a not so silent warning. "Give it a rest and listen. I don't want Ellen hurt."

"Hurt?" Breccan's nostrils flared. "Who wants to hurt Ellen?" He practically vibrated with rage.

Kai sighed. Damn wolves, hot under the collar and too dumb to pay attention. "Just listen. When I was in town yesterday there was talk about Ellen, and you. I'm surprised you haven't had Ellen's dad here with a shotgun, or her pastor. Maybe since you're a shifter they'll cut you some slack, but not much longer. I know you're Ellen's mate and I know that's more permanent than marriage. But not to Ellen's family and friends. And probably not to Ellen. In her family's eyes, she's living in sin. Every time she goes to town she hears it."

"But Ellen's happy. She hasn't said anything about marriage. What do you know about it anyway?" Breccan bristled, fur sprouting on his arms.

"I've known Ellen since she was born. I recommended this place to her when the old man living here wanted to sell to move in with his son. I've seen her teary eyed at church when some of her friends started getting married. There's no mistaking that look. Ellen wants to be married. You just need to ask her. Mating is permanent, but Ellen's not a shifter, so she equates marriage with permanence."

"Ellen doesn't think mating is forever?" Breccan

growled. "Ellen knows it's permanent. I made sure. And she's a shifter now too, even if she hasn't changed yet."

"I don't think she looks at it as marriage, is all. She's not a born shifter. Mating to humans *is* marriage. But there aren't too many of us here, so it has never really been an issue. Do you really want Ellen to have to defend herself every time she goes to town?"

"No." Breccan glared. "Are you sure? Why hasn't Ellen said anything? How do you know this?"

"They talk to me when I go into town." Kai shrugged and said drily, "More like try to pump me for information. I've been here for so many years I'm one of them. I'm not sure most of them even think of me as a shifter."

"Hmm, if I marry Ellen this will stop?"

"Yes."

Breccan turned away. "Hmpf." He looked back over his shoulder as he headed to the house. "Thanks."

****

Connie enjoyed the warmth and scent of the cup in

her hands. Too lazy to get dressed, she was enjoying the quiet morning, drinking a cup of coffee when Ellen danced into the room. She squealed and threw her arms around Connie. "He asked me to marry him! I'm so happy!"

"Whoa! Let me put down my cup before we get burnt!" Connie set her cup down and squeezed Ellen back. "That's great! When did he ask? You didn't mention it last night."

Ellen turned red. "Umm, this morning."

Connie snickered. "Why the red face? Hmm, I bet the real question should be where."

Blushing Ellen laughed. "In the shower. I'm so happy. Since you're here, you'll help me plan it, right?"

"Of course. It's not like we haven't planned our weddings since we were little or anything!" Connie grinned. "This makes my day. I was wondering what I was going to do here. And since you seem to have cornered the hunks in town here on your farm." Thinking of the view she saw yesterday added, "Or at least most of them, there's nothing else for me to do."

Ellen hugged Connie again. "It'll be just like when

we were little."

Connie snorted. "At least you won't be marrying the dog." They both broke down in giggles. The poor dog was always the groom as their brothers flat out refused to play with them. Her eyes widened. "Wait! Oh, my God, I suppose you still are!"

"You're bad!" Ellen swatted her arm, but the giggles didn't stop.

Breccan and Maxwell watched the two of them from the doorway. "How about some breakfast around here?" Breccan was grinning, Max's face held a slight smile.

Connie figured Max heard the news already. She covered her mouth, each time she looked at Breccan, trying to stifle her amusement.

"Connie, do you want an omelet?" Ellen asked, trying, and failing to put on a straight face.

Max headed over and started cracking eggs. He looked completely at home breaking the fragile shells against the bowl. Connie couldn't help but admire him. A hunk and he cooked too. Too bad he wasn't available.

"Please. Before the two of them eat you out of

house and home as big as they are." Connie smirked, watching a couple of dozen eggs make their way into the bowl. "Are you sure Max isn't available? I'd take him off your hands. Save yourself some grocery money."

"No can do." Grinning Ellen started chopping the ham, tomatoes, onions, and spinach. In one frying pan, she added bacon while adding the ingredients to the eggs Max whipped. Turning the bacon over so it didn't burn, Ellen then turned back to the omelet to remove it and start another one. Connie laughed. It was obvious this was a familiar routine.

"I can't believe you're cooking. And not burning anything either."

Ellen tried glaring at Connie, but the smile on her face wouldn't go away, making it less than effective. "I cook every day. I don't know why, these two usually grab something before I do. I swear they eat a cow or pig a day!"

Connie's stomach rolled at that information. "Um, Ellen, TMI!"

Shaking her head Ellen laughed. Connie rolled her eyes and took another sip of her coffee.

"So, Ellen, you still carrying mail?" Perhaps a change in topic would get that visual out of her head.

"Um hm, once a week. I usually work Saturdays. Or when they call for help. It's a nice check, rainy day money or some to splurge once in a while. Why?"

"Know of any veterinarians in town? I want to look for a job. I need to since I had to give up my internship at Brookfield and I need something for the rest of the summer. I planned on studying exotics, but there probably isn't one in town that does that."

"Don't know about that, but there are three vets in town. We can go check them out later this morning if you want." Ellen passed the plates out and sat down to eat. "Why did you have to give up your internship at Brookfield? You've wanted that forever. What gives?"

Connie looked at Ellen. "I'm not ready to discuss it yet." She sighed. "Give me a couple of days, okay? It's crazy and you're not even going to believe it. I'm not really sure how it all happened myself yet. Or truly what happened." Shaking her head Connie tasted the omelet in front of her. The cheese, of course there was cheese on it in Wisconsin, melted in her mouth. It went perfectly with the tang of the tomatoes and the crunchy peppers. "Yum." Connie stuffed more of it in her mouth.

The trio sat, plates overloaded with massive omelets. The men dug in, while Ellen ate a bit daintier. She gave Connie a long look as she slid a loaded fork in her mouth. "Okay. I can give you some time. But I'm warning you, not much, cuz." Ellen grinned. "Besides, we'll have plenty to keep us busy planning the wedding."

The girls looked at each other and started laughing. "Right. So much to plan." Connie bet Ellen could put her hands on wedding planning folders for every wedding they'd ever dreamed of. One year their dream white knights were featured, another surfers. Connie wasn't sure they'd ever planned a wedding with a wolf shifter, but seeing the loving glances between Ellen and Breccan assured her it would be the winner.

The men looked at each other, their puzzlement obvious. It was obvious they had no idea their favorite pastime was planning their weddings. Every time they got together for any length of time they updated them. Before the men could ask the question that was clearly in their eyes, a knock on the kitchen door heralded the man

Connie drooled over the day before at the stoplight. Her breath caught. She could feel her heart race and stomach clench. Looking at him up close, Connie wanted nothing more than to jump his bones. Just the thought of it made her flush.

Kai took a deep breath and froze. He turned and looked straight into her eyes. He took another deep breath, and Connie swore she could see his body vibrate.

Connie's eyes widened. "Ellen, this isn't another one of your men, is it?" she whispered. A stirring of jealousy nudged her at the thought.

A peal of laughter came from Ellen, while Breccan growled. "No, of course not. This is my foreman, Kai. Kai, this is my cousin Connie."

"Hi." Connie smiled appreciatively at Kai, her heart beating erratically. "Ellen, do you have all the good looking men in town on your place?" The jealousy gone, she could feel his pull. So not what she needed right now.

"Hello." Kai grinned at Connie. "So, this is where you were heading?" He came over and leaned down, grabbing her hand, lifting it to his mouth. His lips were soft, lightning streaked through her body at the touch of his lips against her skin. Connie wanted to drown in the sensation, a shiver spreading across her body.

Connie tugged her hand from his and nodded. "I decided to come visit Ellen. I needed to get away from the city for a bit." A shadow passed over her face. Seeing it, Kai gazed intently into her eyes. All the men reacted, their spines straightening and eyes sharpening, all looking at Connie.

Kai pulled Connie into his body, wrapping his steely arms around her. "What's wrong? What are you scared of?"

Connie gasped and wriggled away. Her nipples tightened beneath her thin robe and pajamas. She wouldn't look down. She didn't want to know if they were obvious.

"Nothing. Well, something. I can't talk about it yet. I don't really know how to explain it." She shook her head, frustrated that he'd known she hid something. Ignoring her haywire hormones that thought being wrapped around him perfectly fine, she plopped back down in her chair. "Let me get it straight. I already asked Ellen to give me a couple of days. You guys are just going to have to wait also."

"You can explain it now." Hands on his hips, every inch of Kai demanded an answer.

Connie glared up into Kai's eyes. "Well excuse me, Mr. Bossy Pants. Since I don't know you, you have no say in what I do or don't do." Who did he think he was? He had no right to question her. None. "I'm going to get dressed." Connie flounced up, moving to avoid touching Kai. Gah, even his name was sexy.

Kai moved to block Connie in, obviously riled. She pushed him away, ignoring the warm firm muscles beneath her hands. Before he could reply, Ellen spoke.

"Kai, leave my cousin alone. She'll explain when she's ready." She sighed. "And really, she is nothing to you. Why are you being so bossy? I've never seen you so, so...I don't know..."

Maxwell snorted. "Territorial is the word you want."

"Definitely territorial." Breccan smirked at Kai. "What's up with that, Kai? I never thought a woman would shake that Draconian exterior of yours."

Ellen shook her head, frowning.

Kai turned, glaring at Ellen's mates.

Connie rolled her eyes. It looked like a testosterone fest was going to start in the kitchen. Men could be such idiots. No matter how hot they were.

"Don't start," he growled. Both Maxwell and Breccan wore big grins. Their looks mischievous, obviously ready to tease Kai.

"What's the matter, Kai?"

Kai growled at them again, his eyes starting to glow.

"Holy crap! What the hell is wrong with you?" Connie said, backing up.

Kai whipped his head toward her. She looked totally unsettled. His eyes dropped, taking in the purple silky bathrobe that caressed her curves down to her bare feet and purple toe nails. His nostrils flared in appreciation.

"Nothing." Kai stepped close enough to her to let her feel the heat emanating from his body, his hard, sexy body. Crap! She couldn't think like that. He ran a finger down the side of her cheek, sending a shiver down her spine.

"Back off, bucko!" Connie leaned in, almost touching him. If she touched him, she might not stop. She glared up at him, grinding her teeth. She barely came to his shoulder. It was so much more effective when she wore her heels and could look eye to eye. Her temper sparked, even heels wouldn't help. "I don't know what your problem is. No matter how hot you are, you have no rights over me!"

Connie stamped her foot. Kai looked at her and slowly smiled, heat filling his eyes. Realizing what she said, Connie growled and stomped out of the room followed by his laughter.

CHAPTER THREE

She would make a magnificent dragon. Wrapped in all the gold he could give her, her flesh peeking from beneath. She was his.

"Kai."

He looked over at Ellen, lifting a brow in inquiry.

"Don't mess with my cousin."

He grinned. "I'm not. She's my mate." Ellen's eyes widened while Breccan and Maxwell snickered. His eyes wandered down the hall she'd flounced out. She might have meant to look fierce, but her bouncy blonde hair and petite size negated that. Kai wanted nothing more than to follow her and claim her. Her scent was even stronger in the enclosed space than wafting on the breeze. He'd bet she wore a dragon's mark somewhere on her luscious body. He couldn't wait to hunt for it.

"Holy cow! Are you sure?" Ellen grinned. "That's great!"

Breccan chimed in. "By her reaction, I'd say not so great." He sported a big grin on his face. "Looks like Kai will have a battle on his hands."

Maxwell's sly twist of his lips showed he was enjoying the situation too.

Kai glared at them. Damn wolves. They were a pain. He could see the colors in the kitchen change as his dragon attempted to get out. A little barbeque wolf was a tasty snack. The rumble of agreement by his dragon made him smirk. He couldn't hurt those two, no matter how aggravating they were. Breccan was the only reason Ellen didn't spend her days wrapped in fear any more. His dragon reluctantly settled down.

"What do you mean by that?" Ellen frowned, looking from her mate to him. He could tell Ellen had no idea his dragon was riled, but the smirk on Breccan's face and the rolling of Max's eyes assured him they knew. Damn wolves.

Maxwell looked at Ellen, slinging an arm over her shoulder, chucking her under the chin. "Ellen, did Connie seem thrilled? She didn't even seem to like him, let alone want to be his mate."

Kai growled at his statement.

Ellen swatted at his arm, moving away from Max frowning.

He knew the wolves smelled her arousal. Despite the words that flowed from her soft, pink lips, his mate wanted him. His dragon preened at that fact. She just needed to be around him a bit more. Kai was sure he'd be able to change her mind. They were meant to be together after all.

"But if he's her mate..."

"Ellen." She looked at Breccan. He looked and sounded exasperated. "She has no idea he's her mate. She doesn't know him. It's a different situation than ours. You loved me since you met me and she's just met him." He grinned a bit evilly, obviously enjoying Kai's upcoming problems. "Connie has no idea she's his mate. He's going to have to persuade her, and something tells me it won't be easy."

Ellen looked from her mate to his brother. Kai could tell from the grins on their faces they would enjoy his struggle. He ground his teeth together just thinking of it.

"Whatever. Connie and I are going into town for a bit." Ellen shook her head.

"What for?" Kai asked.

Ellen rolled her eyes. "She wants a job at one of the veterinarians in town. We're going to visit them so she can apply. Does that meet with your approval?"

He ignored the wolves' snickers. Kai knew Connie was meant to be his. Fate was on his side. Kai looked at Ellen and spoke to her mate. "It seems someone has a smart mouth. Maybe you should take care of that."

Ellen snorted.

"I like her mouth." Breccan tossed back. He wagged his eyebrows.

Ellen blushed. "Kai, what did you originally come in for? I think we've gotten way off topic."

"I came in to let you know I picked up the truck yesterday and the men are moving the cattle to the far field for rotation. We'll be harvesting the winter wheat in the next couple of days. I wanted to show Breccan and Maxwell how to do it." He looked at them. "You did say you wanted to learn, right?"

They nodded their heads in agreement.

"Isn't it too early?" Maxwell checked his phone, swiping the screen.

Kai assumed he looked at the calendar on it. When they'd first arrived, Kai told them the normal planting schedule. The heat forced early germination and growing. He was happy to see that Maxwell obviously checked it.

"It is, but it's ready. We might even be able to plant soybeans once we harvest. We should maximize the potential of the land. I have a feeling this is going to be a hard year."

"If you think it's best." Ellen snuggled against Breccan.

"Yes. It can't hurt." Kai glanced at Ellen. He needed more information from his mate and Ellen could get it for him. "Ellen," he said softly. "Find out what has Connie scared. I have a feeling we need to know."

Ellen nodded her agreement and Kai reluctantly

left. No use staying there. Maybe a little space would temper the urgency rushing through his veins. His dragon rumbled, wanting his mate. Kai waited a long time for her. A little longer wouldn't hurt a thing. He ignored the huff from his dragon. He could no longer pluck a mate from the ground and fly away with her. Despite his desire to do so.

Pulling his attention from the thoughts of his mate, Kai headed to the barn. His mate planned on staying, at least for the foreseeable future. She would be here when he finished his chores. Now more than ever, it was imperative to get Breccan and Maxwell trained to take over.

****

Dressed to balance the heat, trying to look professional enough to apply for a job, Connie and Ellen headed into town. Connie lowered the top on the convertible before they took off down the drive.

Ellen tied her hair into a ponytail to try and contain it. "I wondered why you braided your hair! You could have given me some warning!" Ellen laughed. "I thought it was to make a nice impression at the vets."

Connie grinned at her. "Come on, you saw I drove the convertible. It's too nice of a day to leave the top up. If you weren't so preoccupied, you'd have figured it out. Now, I really need a job. Direct me to the closest vet's and we'll go from there."

"Okay. But why do you need a job? What happened with Brookfield?"

"Ellen, I just had to leave, okay? I'll tell you about it later." She glanced at Ellen from the corner of her eye. "Now give, Kai is not off limits, right? He's available?" Connie rolled her eyes at Ellen's giggling. "I know, he's super bossy! I get that. But he's so hot!"

"Well, he's definitely not off limits. Not as far as I know. Maybe with you to concentrate on, Kai will stop bossing me around. I don't need more than Breccan doing that and Maxwell is almost as bad and he's not even my mate." Ellen wrinkled her nose. "I never really thought of Kai as hot. Ewww! I've known him forever!"

"Then how do I not know him?" Connie glanced at Ellen, happy to see the smile on her cousin's face. "Or do

I just not remember him?"

"He's a friend of Grandpa's. They've been friends most of Grandpa's life."

"Ewww. Seriously? How old is he? I thought maybe late twenties, early thirties."

Ellen laughed. "Um, Connie, Kai is a shifter. He's probably older than Grandpa. He's the one that told me Mr. Casey was selling and said he'd help me learn the ropes. He's been helping on the farm for like, forever."

"No way!" Connie looked over at Ellen. "Older than Grandpa? Again, ewww." She sighed. "But he's soooo hot. I don't remember him. I don't remember any shifters here when we lived here." Her eyes widened, the wind, sun and company relaxing her. "That's why his eyes glowed, isn't it?"

Ellen laughed and nodded her head. "Connie there's always been shifters here. Remember Andre from our class? He's some sort of shifter. And the Mackenzie triplets? Boy, they were hot too, remember?"

Connie snorted. "They were total dogs! Always sniffing after the girls. You thought they were hot? They must be at least ten years older than us! I didn't realize you were such a horn dog as a little girl!" Connie shook her head with a smile.

"No, silly!" Ellen laughed. "They were friends with my brother Hank! I've known them my whole life. I've seen the men they've become and Connie, they are to die for." She shivered. "But they are no way more gorgeous than Breccan."

"Well, he's hunkalicious! Max too. But I think Kai has them beat." Connie shivered remembering the feel of his firm muscles beneath her hand, against her body. "There is just something about him."

Connie wanted to hug herself. Nothing was more fun than gossiping about men, hot touchable men. She so needed this visit, despite the circumstances. Her life lately full of studying and totally devoid of fun.

"At the next corner turn left. One of the vet's is about a block up. He's the newest vet, so he might have an opening." They were almost to town. Since the town was so small, it surprised her there were three veterinarians.

Connie followed directions and pulled into the lot. "Wow! Look at this place." Her jaw dropped. It was huge. Connie gestured to the front. "Animal Kingdom, huh? Maybe I'll be able to do exotics here." It appeared to anchor the small strip mall, taking up more than half of the frontage. She hoped there was a vacancy. Being newly opened, the veterinarian should have the latest equipment. She could only hope. Connie hopped out of the car. "Wish me luck!"

Ellen followed behind her. "I'm going over to the coffee shop next door. Meet me when you get done."

Connie nodded, entering the door. A small bell tinkled overhead, giving notice that someone entered the building. The waiting room was super clean, a large bird cage off to the side with a decidedly ratty looking macaw in it. Connie chuckled, below the cage, a pack of kittens stared hungrily at it. The bird would make mincemeat of the little guys. They just didn't realize it. A young man in scrubs entered the room. He sauntered up to the counter.

"How may I help you?" He leaned toward her, sniffing discreetly, and peered over the counter, searching for an animal. "Are you here to pick up?"

"No. My name is Connie. I'm a veterinary student and I wondered if there were any openings?"

He got a big grin on his face at her explanation. "Have a seat. I'm Lou. Let me get the doc." He turned and without moving shouted, "Doc, we got a live one here! Move it before she leaves!"

Connie stifled a laugh and rolled her eyes. Informal as all veterinarian offices appeared to be. Connie stood up, jaw dropping as the 'Doc' came into view.

Doc was gorgeous. He laughed looking at her face. He stepped forward to shake her hand and frowned. He appeared to be sniffing the air around her.

"What?" Connie narrowed her eyes, looking back and forth from the doc and Lou. "What is up with all the sniffing around here? I took a shower for goodness sake!"

Lou laughed, while the veterinarian grinned. "You're not a shifter, but you've been around them recently." Doc sniffed again, a tiny frown between his eyes. "Who have you been around?"

Connie frowned. "Does it really matter?"

"It may. Some don't want their women around other shifters."

She rolled her eyes. Like anyone had a claim on her. Not.

"Oh, for Pete's sake! I don't have anyone to dictate to me. I'm staying with my cousin, and her mate and his brother are shifters. That's probably who you smell."

"I smell a dragon shifter."

She grimaced. "Breccan and Maxwell are wolf shifters. I don't know any dragon shifters." She shifted impatiently. She didn't know for sure what kind of shifter Kai was, but why wouldn't he be a wolf? They were notoriously territorial. "I only came in to see if you had any openings. If you don't, I'll check another vet."

Connie realized even though the doc was drop dead handsome, he still didn't affect her like Kai. She looked him in the eye. She was not about to back down or crawl out of the office. He leaned in closer and sniffed again. A slow grin split his face. Hmm. She wondered what that was about.

"I have an opening. I was getting ready to call UW for a student. The intern I scheduled, cancelled on me last week."

Connie's stomach leaped. She didn't want to lose

this opportunity despite the sniffing thing.

He gestured toward the back. "Follow me, so I can go over your information and you can fill out an application." He turned and Connie followed behind him, heartened when Lou gave her a thumbs up.

Application filled out, and an impromptu interview behind her, Connie stood.

"I think you'll do fine here, Connie. Welcome aboard."

"Thank you. Thank you so much." Butterflies filled her middle. She got the job. She couldn't wait to start.

Connie shook hands with Doc, ecstatically happy. He grinned and to her surprise enveloped her in a big hug, rubbing his chin on top of her hair. Connie struggled, pulling back, frowning. Even though it seemed a brotherly hug, almost a noughie when he rubbed her hair, she needed to make sure he didn't get any funny ideas. Her stomach sank. She really wanted this job. It gave her the chance to study exotics and paid well too. But not if the doc thought he could get handsy.

"Doc, I really want this job, but I'm not willing to

do anything else. I'm not sure this is going to work." She frowned at him, hands on her hips.

"No problem." He grinned. "The dragon shifter scent I smell is not one of the shifters you mentioned. I recognize it now. I just wanted him to know I met you. So, he could come say hi."

"Care to enlighten me?" Connie sniffed, a bit miffed. Why would hugging her make anyone go to the vets? She shook it off. Shifters were beginning to seem just a bit strange.

"No. I'll see you next week." He held open the door, shaking her hand. "Nice to have you onboard Connie."

"Thank you." She smiled and waved at Lou, who grinned at her from behind the counter. She turned and headed to the coffee shop. Ellen waited for her there. She danced a jig on the sidewalk. She got the job! Time to find Ellen and share her news.

Connie burst through the doors of the coffee shop with a huge smile. "Ellen, I got the job!" She plopped down on a chair. "I'll be able to help with exotics. Some, at any rate. He says that he does birds and the occasional reptile." She motioned with a hand. "It's definitely better than I could have expected."

Ellen squealed. "That's great! When do you start?"

"Monday! I'm so happy we came. He said he was getting ready to call the UW veterinary school for an intern. Talk about luck!" Connie was practically dancing in her seat the more she talked. "I've all the qualifications he was looking for. He said I can start out at four hours a day. If he likes what I do, he'll make it six to eight hours a day! That will totally fill my requirement! He knew my professor, and he said it shouldn't be any problem to get full credit, even though I'm out of state." She jumped up. "Come on. Let's grab a frappe to go." Her thoughts were in a swirl. Happiness zinged through her. Excitement made her whole day brighter. "We should go to the church to reserve a date for your wedding, too."

Ellen laughed but it sounded brittle to Connie's ears. "Sure thing." She didn't stand up though.

Connie knew when she got hyped up, it was like trying to stop a steam roller. She just couldn't seem to stop herself. She dropped her head. "Crap. You probably want to do that with Breccan."

Connie took a good look at Ellen. Color in her cheeks and a happy smile on her face, yet there was still a fragile look to her eyes. "What's the matter, Ellen?" Connie closed her eyes, ashamed of herself. It couldn't be, could it? "Ellen, is this the first time you've been out without Breccan or Maxwell?"

Ellen tentatively nodded. Closed her eyes and whispered, "It's hard, Connie." She smiled a bit. "But, today… today I came in here all by myself. No one with me and the guys weren't here." She looked at Connie. "It was kind of scary, but I did it." Her smile widened. "It was the first time I went somewhere, anywhere, other than work, by myself." She threw her arms around Connie, smiling and crying. "It feels so damn good!"

Connie hugged her back. It was a punch to her chest. They stood there, laughing and crying, arms locked around each other. Connie could feel the joy emanating from her cousin. She caught her breath, wanting to just cry for her cousin. Wanting to murder the man that hurt her and made her scared to walk into a coffee shop by herself. Thoughtless as she had been, it was evidently something Ellen needed to do.

Connie's neck prickled. She caught a man watching them and frowned. He looked familiar. She ignored the feeling when he turned back to his newspaper, ignoring them. Their squealing must have disturbed him.

"Well, come on, I want an iced coffee, girl. I'm dying here!" Arm in arm, they headed to the counter to order. After paying and thanking the woman, they turned to leave.

"I wish you would move back home." Ellen held the door open. "I have a feeling we're going to have fun." She giggled. "Probably more than any of the guys will want."

Connie aimed her key fob at the car. She heard the sound of the locks opening. "Probably! At least I don't have a watchdog looking over my every move." They both laughed as they got into the car. The heat oppressive. Connie struggled to breathe, wishing they were back in the air conditioning. She took a long pull of her frappe. When had she become such a wimp?

"Ya think? Didn't look like that this morning." Ellen snickered, slurping her iced coffee.

"Shut up, Ellen." It was a halfhearted response. Connie put her drink in the cup holder and backed up. "I don't know what his problem is, but he'd better get over it and fast." Kai's possessive tone both thrilled and repulsed her. Pulling forward to exit the parking lot, Connie asked, "Still St. Catherine's?"

Ellen smiled. "Yup. Remember how to get there?" St. Catherine's the scene of many a young drama. How could she forget?

"Jeez Ellen, it hasn't been that long. How often did we have to walk there for catechism when our brothers ditched us?" She shook her head. "Like all the time!"

CHAPTER FOUR

Kai heard the car pull in. Connie and Ellen laughing as they sped down the long driveway, rocks spitting out from beneath the tires. He shook his head, grinning. Connie appeared to be a bit of a speed demon. Their laughter floated on the breeze. The sound caught Breccan's attention too. He turned to Kai.

"I figure we're done for the day, right?"

Kai nodded. "Yes." He smiled and started cleaning up his tools.

"Why don't you take supper with us tonight?" Breccan's grin devilish. He headed over to open the garage doors. Maxwell and Breccan converted the old carriage house into a garage once they moved in.

Kai just looked at him, deadpan. "Don't mind if I do. Just ring the bell when dinner's done." He had enough will power to wait for dinner. Despite the eagerness of his dragon to see her again. Really, he did.

The girls pulled up to the garage, Breccan meeting them. Ellen hopped out. Connie pulled forward, driving her convertible inside the darkened interior. Breccan closed the doors and Kai could hear a muffled 'Hey!' from Connie. Breccan and Ellen were laughing and he swept Ellen off her feet and headed in the house.

Maxwell met them at the door, holding it open and letting it slam shut behind him before heading to the barn.

Kai headed toward the garage, his will power gone. He opened the door and stepped inside.

"Finally. Turn on the light so I can see you turkeys!" Connie projected, a lilt in her voice.

Kai switched on the flickering lights.

She got out of the car and stood up, spying him. "Oh!" Her voice was breathless.

She closed the car door and Kai was right there.

He couldn't stay away. He stepped closer, trapping her against the side of the car. He placed his hands on the door, engulfing her in his embrace without touching her. He leaned in and breathed her scent deeply into his lungs and suddenly froze. Straightening up, stepping closer so his body was imprinted on hers, he placed a hand on the back of her neck. He breathed deeply again, and glared.

"Where the hell were you?" His hand tightened on her neck. "Who were you with?" He looked down into her eyes. Cerulean blue, deep enough to lose himself in, gazed up at him in confusion and irritation. Kai took a deep breath. Calm. Another. Not there yet.

He breathed out through his nose. He didn't want to alienate her. But her fire was enticing.

"What are you talking about? And again, what business is it of yours?" Irritation was winning out over confusion.

Kai realized he needed to reign in his temper. He gentled his hand, stroking her neck with his thumb. Kai could feel her shiver even though she tried to hide it. His lips quirked and her reaction settled him. "I'm sorry." She looked amazed he apologized, startling a bark of laughter from him. "How was your day?"

She still gave him a dirty look, obviously not letting him sweet talk her. "It was fine." She brightened up. "I got a job! The vet hired me on a trial basis." She smiled. "Isn't that fantastic?"

He grinned ruefully down at her, his smile lopsided. He was an ass. He knew it. She had a right to be happy. If she was happy, she'd stay. "That is good news. So, you'll be moving here?"

Connie shook her head and settled back against the car. "No. I still have to finish school. I need an internship before I can graduate. I'll be here for the summer, though."

Kai nodded, his insides tight. He had the summer to convince her to stay. He leaned down and sniffed her hair. She'd definitely been around a shifter, a dragon shifter, and he recognized the scent. He ignored the scent of the other; the prey wasn't worth worrying over.

"What is up with the sniffing?" She sounded aggravated.

"What do you mean?"

"You sniffed me, Lou sniffed me, and the doc

sniffed me. I took a shower! So, what the heck is going on?"

Kai grinned, a laugh rumbling out of his chest. Eyes spitting fire at him, Connie shoved at him to push him away. He didn't budge. Kai grabbed her hands, one large hand pinning them down against the car and leaned down to kiss her. He took his time, tracing her soft lips with his tongue before plunging his inside to taste her sweetness. Her flavor burst on his tongue.

Connie struggled at first, and then tilted her head, opening her mouth to further exploration. He deepened the kiss, the softness of her mouth addicting.

Kai released her hands and pulled Connie up against him. Her arms slipped around his neck pulling him down as he pulled her up. Kai ran his hands up and down her back, pulling her legs around his waist. He rumbled. The feel of her curvy body against him drove him crazy. He moved, the denim constricting his erection. His dragon surfaced, wanting to claim her. He pulled her tighter against him, nestling his cock between the warmth he could feel emanating from between her legs. Kai rubbed against her, seeking relief. He wanted nothing more than to burst free and enter that sanctuary his denim denied him.

Connie pulled from his kiss with a gasp and buried her face in his neck. Her warm breath caressed his skin, raising the hair on the back of his neck. His arms tightened around her, his hands caressing her bottom.

"Oh, my goodness." She sounded breathless. "You're lethal."

Kai chuckled, the vibration making her nipples harden against him even more. He could smell her arousal. Pretty sure if he pushed it, he could strip her and take her right here. His cock throbbed at the thought. But that's not how he wanted to have her the first time, on her car, in the garage with Ellen, Maxwell and Breccan just outside the door. Because damn it, he could hear them. He thought they went into the house for a while.

Kai kissed the top of her hair. He loosened her arms to let her go. She tightened her arms and legs around him and kept her face buried in his neck. It didn't appear she wanted to move. He squeezed her, hugging his treasure to him. A sense of peace settled over him. This is what he searched so long for. His treasure. His future. He turned and leaned against the car. He'd hold her as long as she let him. His hands were filled, cupping her ass, and holding her tight against his cock, torture, but sweet all the same.

"Connie, you coming out?" Ellen banged against the door and Kai could hear her laughing. Connie stirred, raising her head. Kai leaned forward and kissed her softly, just enough to taste her sweetness.

"Yes, I am. Give me a minute." She groaned, dropping her head against her chest.

"Ready to get down?" Kai loosened his arms, letting Connie unhook her legs, holding her until he was sure she could stand on her own.

"Um." Connie stared up at him. Kai flashed a grin. She still looked a little dazed, a bit unsure. He didn't think that was normal for the little spitfire.

Her eyes narrowed at his grin. There she was.

"I think we're done here." She snorted, turned, and flounced away.

His grin widened. Yes, flounced was the only word for it.

"For now." He'd let her walk away, but she needed

to know they weren't done. Not by a long shot.

She turned and glared, but it seemed only half-hearted. She slammed the door. Kai chuckled, adjusting his cock before leaving the garage. This was definitely going to be an enjoyable summer.

****

Connie shook her head shutting the door. A small grin slipped across her mouth. This summer just became interesting. She looked up. Ellen was standing there with a grin on her face.

"Soooo. What took so long?" Judging by her smile Ellen knew something was up.

That would have been Kai. She snickered.

"Nothing. Kai just helped me out of the car."

"Just the car, huh?" Ellen looked like she didn't believe her. "Not your panties, eh?" She laughed.

"Ellen! Jeez! Just because you're a horn dog, doesn't mean everyone else is."

Ellen laughed. "Since when have you become a prude?"

"I'm not! Nosy, much?"

"All right, I'll stop. For now." Ellen chuckled. "Come on, we have some wedding planning to do."

"By the way, is Kai a wolf shifter too?"

Ellen snorted. "Not by half. He's a dragon."

Connie gasped. She'd no idea how to respond. One half thrilled he was such a dominant animal, the other half appalled, and for the same reason. Confused didn't begin to describe her state of mind.

They headed toward the house to work on wedding plans. Connie looked back over her shoulder when she heard the garage door open. Kai came out. His eyes met Connie's. She could feel a flush come over her body, sending a shiver down her spine, at the heat in his eyes. Flustered, she turned away, and entered the house. A dragon. What was she going to do?

"Get your laptop, Connie. I've got mine set up in the kitchen."

"Sure thing." Connie headed into her bedroom to grab it. She entered, shut the door and leaned against it. She took a deep breath and let it out in a whoosh. She shuddered, just thinking of him. Her nipples still hard and her panties drenched. Ellen was right; if he tried he could have her out of them without a fight or whimper.

She pushed off the door and headed to the bathroom. Connie grabbed a washcloth and getting it nice and wet, wrung it out and swiped it across her burning face and neck. Drying off, she quickly changed, grabbed her laptop, and headed into the kitchen.

Ellen's laptop was already on the table.

"Hey. I thought for sure you'd grab a cold shower." Ellen glanced over at Connie with a smirk.

"Oh, shut up!"

Ellen laughed. "I'm getting dinner ready real quick. I figured we'd barbeque, since it's so hot. Breccan's lighting the grill and Maxwell is grabbing some corn from the garden. I've got some steaks here that should work for all of us and I figured I'd toss a salad."

"Sounds good. Did you tell him you setup the wedding date?"

"Yup," Ellen nodded. "He was fine with it. When I told them we went to my parents to let them know the date, Breccan didn't seem to have a problem with it." She opened the refrigerator grabbing a bunch of green stuff.

Connie laughed. "Unlike your mom and dad! I guess we should have brought him with."

"He really seemed to be okay with me telling them by myself. He just asked if that was the soonest we could get married." Connie snorted.

"What's the rush?"

Ellen rolled her eyes tearing apart the lettuce. "He mentioned me being his officially. Maxwell added then he would own me. As if."

Connie snickered. "Seriously? He said that?"

Ellen nodded.

"Did you whack him?"

Ellen sniggered. "Of course, I tried! But Breccan must have realized I was going to smack him and pulled Max out of the way. Then they headed outside." She snorted. "I could see Breccan yelling at him the whole way!" Both of them giggled at that.

"You finish making the salad. I'll go online and pull up wedding dresses." Connie typed in the information and then looked up, gazing out the kitchen window. Kai stood at the doors to the barn, pulling off his shirt. Her stomach twisted at the sight. His back was as muscular as his chest and abdomen were. It was dark in the barn, but she caught flashes of white. She wasn't sure, but it looked like he was undressing. She heard Ellen laugh. When he disappeared from sight Connie sighed and looked up at Ellen. "What?"

"What were you looking at?"

"Nothing. What's in the barn?" Ellen got a big smile on her face.

"Why don't you go look? We have time before dinner."

"No, that's all right." No way did she want to go in the barn. Kai would think she followed him. He was cocky enough. "Maybe I'll check it out later. You don't have a whole lot of time before your wedding and we have to find your dress."

"Are you sure? Kai wouldn't mind if you joined him." Ellen's snicker lit her temper.

Connie's face flushed. "Dammit Ellen, I am not going to chase that man!" She glared at her. "He has enough confidence without me following him around!"

Ellen chuckled and finished the salad. "Connie,

you're fighting a losing battle. But go right ahead. I'm sure it will be fun to watch!"

"What. Ever."

"All right, all right! I'll leave it alone." Ellen raised her hands in defeat. "There, everything we need is ready until the grill is done. Let's look at dresses. But I want to see if Grandma's will fit."

"Do you have it?"

"It's in the attic. My mom brought it over a while ago."

They skimmed sites, saving the ones they liked. Laughing and joking about others. The girls looked up at noise coming from the door. All three men entered, stamping feet and tossing hats into the mudroom. Connie sighed and whispered.

"Boy, Ellen that sure is a good looking bunch." The men all looked up and grinned. Connie could feel her face heat. "Oh, my God! Ellen, they heard me!" She laid her head on the table with a thump. Ellen chuckled beside her.

"Um, shifters, Connie. Of course, they heard you."

Connie moaned into the table. The men laughed.

Connie peeked up at Kai and quickly closed her eyes again. He wore a big grin on his face. He really was handsome. She groaned and hid a grin. Sometimes it was just fun playing the drama queen! But how on earth was she going to resist him?

She felt his hand on her neck and jumped slightly. She opened her eyes. Kai's face was right in hers. "Jeez, a little space please!" His hand on her neck sent little tingles down her spine. Her stomach jumped from the warmth of his hand. She hunched over more, not willing to move and not wanting him to know his effect on her.

"You could have joined me in the barn. I saw you watching me."

"Uh, no. What kind of a girl do you think I am?" Connie flushed, heat rising in her cheeks despite not wanting him to see his effect on her.

He grinned at her. "My kind." Connie narrowed her eyes at him. She enjoyed his teasing, but no way was she letting him know that.

"Think again, bucko."

Kai laughed and moved his hand down her back in a slow caress. Connie arched against his hand, enjoying his touch. Ellen and Breccan smothered smiles. Max ignored them all. Connie hung her head. Darn it, the man could make her forget her name. Connie totally forgot they weren't alone. She jumped up. "I'm going to put up my computer. Ellen, shall I move yours too?"

"Please."

CHAPTER FIVE

Connie yawned and stretched. She settled back and thought about last night. Overall, it was a good night. Kai was…Connie sighed. She didn't know what Kai was. But boy did he get her motor running! All the little touches at dinner kept her totally distracted. She grinned. But she had her revenge. It was definitely a two-way street. He got just as worked up, but he hid it better.

Kai even distracted her from why she was in Wisconsin in the first place. She should call Matt, see what was going on. Then she needed to tell Ellen. She got up, brushed her teeth, and headed to the kitchen. First though, coffee.

She got closer, heard Ellen giggle, and the sound of a man's rough whisper. At the doorway, she wasn't surprised to see Ellen sitting in Breccan's lap laughing, a cup of coffee in her hand, while he nibbled on her neck.

"Morning you two," Connie beamed at the glow on Ellen's face.

Ellen looked up, a smile on her face. "Morning. Would you like some breakfast?"

Connie shook her head. "I just want a cup of coffee." She looked at the counter. "Maybe a piece of fruit." She grabbed a coffee mug and added cream. Pouring the coffee, Connie took a deep breath, enjoying the heavenly smell. "Mmm." Connie reached over and grabbed a banana, peeling and eating it against the counter. Tossing the peel in the trash, Connie took a long pull of coffee. "I gotta call Matt."

"You can use the house phone if you want." Ellen watched her. "There's an extension in the living room and one in my computer room."

"You still have a landline? That's okay. I have my cell." She closed her eyes. "I'll just finish my coffee before I call him." Connie leaned against the counter, hands wrapped around her cup. She could see the steam rise from it. She really didn't want to call her brother, but hopefully it would be good news. She sipped and leaned against the counter. She sighed and straightened up. There was no use putting it off. "I'll sit on the porch and make my call."

Connie settled on the swing, setting it to rock with her foot. She sipped her coffee, looking out over the farm. She pulled out her phone and set it down next to her. The call could wait until she finished her coffee. She finished enjoying the peace of the morning, the rocking of the swing soothing. She set her cup down on the porch and sat back up. Pushing off again, setting the swing to rock, Connie picked up her phone. She really didn't want to talk to Matt. She dialed and it rang once before Matt picked it up. Figured. He couldn't let it go to voice mail.

"Hey, Connie is that you?"

"Hi, Matt. Have you found him yet?"

"No, Con. But your apartment was broken into. Did you leave anything that would say where you were going?"

"Um. Let me think. Matt, I think I left my address

book out. I just double checked Ellen's address so I could put it in the GPS." Connie tightened her hand on the phone, her stomach dropped. "Matt, do you think he knows where I'm at? What should I do?"

"I'll check and see if your address book is out. Just in case, I'm going to call the Sheriff's Department there." He sighed. "I don't like the idea of you and Ellen being out there by yourselves. Maybe you two should temporarily move back with Uncle Tom and Aunt Maggie."

"We're not here by ourselves. Remember Ellen's dogs? The guys will protect us." Her temples pounded. Why did this have to happen to her?

"The dogs are definitely big enough, but they're just animals. And what guys are you talking about?"

"Breccan and Maxwell. You know, Ellen's mate and his brother. They're not really dogs, they're wolf shifters. And Kai, he could protect us. He's a shifter too. They're all here at Ellen's place."

"I forgot about that. Hank did say something about them really being shifters. But Kai who? Are you sure you can trust him?"

"Um, yeah. I'm pretty sure. He's a friend of Grandpa's."

"All right. But if there's any problem you call me. We're looking for leads, so hopefully we'll catch him soon."

"Okay, I will. Bye, Matt."

"Bye, Connie. Be careful."

Connie closed her phone and looked up. Kai watched her from the barn. She ducked her head. His eyes burned as they looked at her. She squirmed and realized she was sitting on the porch in her nightie. It wouldn't normally bother her, but Kai's gaze caressed her skin like a physical touch. She ducked her head. She wasn't ready to talk to him yet. Peeking between her lashes, she caught the sly grin aimed in her direction. A man came up to him, obviously with an enquiry and Kai turned away. Connie took this chance to escape. She hopped off the swing and went back into the house.

"Ellen, I'm gonna hop in the shower," Connie passed through the kitchen. Ellen and Maxwell were still sitting at the table talking. Breccan was nowhere in sight.

"All right, Connie." Ellen waved absentmindedly.

Connie headed into her room. The conversation with her brother replaying in her mind. There was nothing she could do about it, except wait and see what happened. She definitely needed to let Ellen and the men know. She grabbed her toiletries, looking out the window. Kai stood near the barn, Breccan at his side, gesturing toward the field. Breccan threw back his head laughing. Kai glanced at the house, glared at Breccan and stomped off. Breccan headed into the barn still chuckling.

Connie shook her head and smiled, then exhaled. Even in a temper, Kai was a fine looking man. She looked down at her hands in disgust. She could not get him out of her head. Hopefully, starting work on Monday, he would take a backseat in her thoughts. Thinking of that, Connie looked around the room. Most of her clothes were hanging out of the dresser, tossed there in a hurry last night while she looked for her swim suit. Looking around she realized she didn't have any scrubs. Tossing her toiletry bag down, Connie decided to put her clothes away then get her scrubs from the trunk of the car. A shower could wait a bit. Putting her iPod on, she danced around the room, cleaning it up.

Satisfied, Connie looked around. Much better. Debating whether or not to change, Connie headed to the garage and her car. She really wanted a shower before she got dressed, so hopefully no one would see her sneak out to it. Her scrubs lived in the trunk of her car. She took them out to the cleaners near her apartment and hadn't gotten around to dropping them off, luckily for her. So, she just grabbed the laundry basket and dumped them in her parent's trunk when she ran. Getting them now, Connie could make sure they were clean and pressed for work on Monday.

Passing through the kitchen, she noticed it was empty. Connie grabbed her keys and headed to the car. Outside she looked around. Kai nowhere in sight. Her body tingled just thinking of him. Shaking her head, she continued to the garage. It was a good thing he wasn't around. Really.

****

Standing just inside the barn, Kai watched Connie slip into the garage, leaving the door ajar. He burned just looking at her. He couldn't resist the chance to spend a few stolen moments with her. He slid quietly into the garage. Connie bent over, looking into her trunk. Her purple baby doll gown so short he oogled the perfect view of the delicate lace of her matching thong running through her cheeks. There it was, the mate mark of a dragon kissing the sweet curve of her left buttock. Kai hardened in an instant. His heart raced, and he salivated at the sight. He watched her rummage around, humming. Glancing into the trunk, his eyes widened. Small as it was, it was full and totally disorganized. He moved closer and peeked over her shoulder.

He realized she hadn't heard him. Her iPod blaring full blast, so loud he could hear the words of the song. Standing behind her, close enough to feel the tempting heat of her body, Connie leaned further down pushing her ass firmly into his groin. Kai groaned, she gasped and froze. Grasping her hips, Kai rubbed against her. His cock seeking the warmth of her body even through his jeans.

Kai's firm hands held her tight against him, his jeans the only barrier against her firm buttocks. His hard length shifted against her and she ground back against him.

Kai slid his hands to the top of Connie's baby doll, the elastic giving him easy access to her breasts. He filled his hands with her luscious curves, pushing them together as his thumbs and forefingers squeezed and tugged her nipples. Connie shuddered. Held in place by his hard body, she could only wriggle her ass against him. Leaving one hand teasing her nipple, he slid his other to her pussy, pulling her back so she wasn't pressing against the edge of the trunk. He didn't want any bruises on her. Kai stroked her slit with his fingers, rubbing her through her thong. He slid his fingers under the silky material, rubbing a callused fingertip against her clit. Soft and wet, his fingers slid easily against her.

Connie squirmed, pushing and rubbing against his groin, denim confined him. He ached, pressing against the unforgiving fabric. Reluctantly releasing her breast, Kai reached his hand down and tore her thong off, leaving her defenseless against him. Kai rubbed her clit with one hand, and pushed the other between her legs to plunge a finger in and out of her tight pussy, her cream easing the way. Hot, smooth silk surrounding his digit. He swelled against her. He could just imagine her tight body strangling him as he slid inside, stretching her to take him. Connie convulsed, constricting his fingers as he rhythmically worked in and out of her. She moaned, clenching his finger, shivering as her orgasm peaked. She drove him wild.

Kai moved one hand to her stomach, pressing Connie against him as he slowly eased his drenched finger from her. He slipped it into his mouth, her flavor bursting over his tongue. He rumbled, wanting more. He could feel Connie tremble. Kai encircled her in his arms, his chest against her back as they both leaned over her rear bumper.

"Kai, I need to stand up." Kai caressed Connie enjoying the feeling of her silky skin. He tugged on a nipple, loving the feel of her in his fingers. She was so soft compared against his callused hands. He gently pulled her up and turned her to face him, pulling her against his chest. She moaned and leaned into him. The feel of her hard nipples against his chest drove him crazy. He should just take her right then and there. His dragon agreed.

"Those were my favorite panties."

He snorted, but didn't reply.

"You can't do this to me."

He grinned at her. He could and would. "Yes. I can." He nuzzled the top of her head.

"No. You need to leave me alone." She pushed futilely at his chest.

Kai firmed his arms around her, enjoying the feel of her against him. "I can't, Connie. You're my mate."

Connie froze. He could feel her heart race at his announcement.

"Connie?" He pulled back and looked down at her.

"I don't think that's such a good idea." She dropped her head against his chest. "I can't be your mate. It's way too scary to even think of, especially now."

"What are you scared of?" He'd just have to show her it was a good idea, the best idea. He wouldn't give her up. He'd searched too long for her. He'd just have to woo her. He slid a hand down, cupping the curve of her buttocks. She shivered. He gloated, but refused to show it. No matter what she said, Connie couldn't resist him.

"I'm afraid I'll have to leave. Heck, I'm afraid I'll want to stay." Connie shook her head. "I don't have time for this, Kai. I'm trying to finish veterinary school. I've got some crazy guy after me. I want to…"

"What crazy guy?" His voice roughened, the thought of her being a victim made him see red. Kai would eliminate the threat. Once he found him, he was a dead man.

"Um." Connie raised her head, looking up at Kai. His eyes were hard, his face serious.

"What crazy guy, Connie?"

She exhaled softly, dropping her head back on his chest. "I came here to get away from Chicago. I was on my way home and at a traffic light, I looked down an alley. It was still daylight, for Pete's sake! I saw what looked like a drug deal, and then this one guy went crazy. He pulled out a gun and shot another guy! I screamed and stepped on the gas to get away. He must have heard me scream. One guy ran after my car. I don't know if they got my license plate or not. I went straight to my brother's. I was so scared." She shivered. Kai's arms tightened around her. He would keep her safe.

"Why didn't you go to the police?"

"I did. My brother's a cop. He took me to the cop shop to report it. Then we went to the DOT to change my license plate, so they couldn't find my car. After that, I looked at some mug shots to see if I could ID him, and they were able to bring him in." She sniffled. "When I went back to do the lineup to identify him, one of his buddies saw me and followed me home. I don't know why he was there, probably just trying to bail the guy out. He must have been there that day and recognized me."

"How did you get away? I'm assuming he didn't follow you here. Did he?"

"No. I left the car he followed in the parking garage, and grabbed some stuff and left in the convertible. It's my parents' but I've been using it occasionally while they're gone."

Kai snorted. More than occasionally would be his guess, based on the contents of the trunk. He ran his hands over her back, trying to soothe her.

"The exit to the parking garage is on the other side of the block, so he didn't see me. But my brother said my apartment was broken into, and I think my address book was on the counter." She shivered. "Open to Ellen's address page. All the families' addresses were on that page."

"So, we can assume they will be looking for you. Was your brother going to contact anyone?" He would have to step up the security at the farm. No one was going to endanger his mate.

"I don't know." Connie snuggled closer to him. "I'm scared. I need to tell Ellen and Uncle Tom and Aunt Maggie to be careful. He couldn't be dumb enough to go after my brothers."

"Let's go do that now. But first, what were you doing out here?" He tightened his arms around her, enjoying the feel of her body against his.

"Oh!" Connie pulled away and turned back to her car. "I needed to bring my scrubs in and wash them." She started pulling out clothes and jammed them into Kai's arms.

He grunted. He'd rather hold her, not some smelly clothing. The aroma of gas and grease mixed with her sweat. It cooled his ardor until she bent into the trunk again. Damn, he'd have a permanent impression of his zipper on his dick.

"Here, hold these while I get them all." Finishing, she grabbed what appeared to be an empty duffle bag. "Here we go. You can put them in here." Kai stuffed the clothes in the bag, a grin on his face. Connie looked up at him. "What's so funny?"

"You jump from mood to mood at the drop of a hat. I have a feeling I'm never going to be bored around you."

She sniffed at him.

"Whatever." Grabbing the bag and looping it over her arm, Connie attempted to leave. Kai grabbed her, pulled her back and kissed her, hard, running his hands over her bare ass, dipping his finger into her slit. She squirmed, bucking against his hand. Connie tore herself from his arms, shaking her head.

"Behave." She was breathless. "Let's go back inside and let everyone know what's going on." Connie pulled up her top, covering her breasts from his view.

Kai grunted, wanting to taste them. Wondering how he neglected the pouty peaks. He reached for them.

Connie backed up, giving him a breathless laugh.

"No." She turned and headed to the door. The duffle held against her. "If you don't want anyone else to see my ass, I suggest you walk behind me."

Kai's eyes widened. How the hell had he not noticed how exposed she was when she came out? No one could see her like this. Kai grunted and moved close. She was his. He'd flame anyone else that saw her like this.

Connie elbowed him.

"Back up a little, so I can walk. Jeez."

Kai grumbled, giving her just a bit of room to move and followed her out. Luckily, no one was in the yard. He wouldn't have to kill any of the hands. Which was good, they'd be hard to replace.

No one was in the kitchen either when they got there. Better yet. He followed her, stopping when she turned, pushing against his chest. They were at her bedroom door.

"Kai, I need to take a shower." She rolled her eyes. "Especially now." She shooed him away with her hands. "Go away. Find Ellen, Breccan and Max, okay?"

"Connie." He took a step forward.

Connie stepped back and closed the door in his face. He growled, not wanting to leave her. Not that she gave him a choice. He ignored the fact she'd smirked as she closed the door. He wanted to please her, and she knew it. Plus, everyone needed to know about the possible danger coming their way. Kai turned and left to search for the others. Adjusting his denims to make himself more comfortable.

CHAPTER SIX

Stepping into the kitchen, Connie drooped. She didn't want to tell them. Kai, Ellen and the guys sat waiting for her. She plopped down in the chair Kai held out for her. No excuses now, she needed to let them know the situation. She'd called Matt for an update after her shower. Hoping for good news. Just the opposite, in fact. Now her whole family was in danger because of her. Breccan shifted in his seat, leaning toward her. Maxwell stood, arms crossed leaning against the counter.

"Ellen, give your folks a call. They need to know too." Connie grimaced. She couldn't believe she was in this situation through no fault of her own.

Brows raised Ellen dialed. "Okay. If you're sure."

Connie nodded.

They answered and after a short conversation Ellen put them on speaker. Connie didn't want to have to explain more than once. Her stomach knotted. This sucked.

"Okay, time to spill," Ellen teased.

Connie took a deep breath and blurted. "I witnessed a murder and now they're after me." The shocked faces and gasps from her aunt and uncle let her know they weren't expected that. "I witnessed a drug deal. Purely by coincidence, at the wrong place at the wrong time. Stupid stop light. I didn't realize what was happening at first. I saw men in an alley, and then I heard gun shots. Instinctively, I turned." She swallowed, fear making her shake. Connie whispered, "It was horrible. I went straight to Matt."

Kai's hands squeezed her shoulders, giving her a bit more confidence. His warm touch made her feel safe. No one spoke. She glanced at him and he nodded.

"The cops picked him up from my description. At the lineup, one of his men was there. They were all gang members. Kind of hard to miss. Anyway, he followed me home. I was scared, so I ran here. I didn't figure they'd find me up here. But..." Her nose stung and her eyes began to burn. She bit her lip.

"But?" Maxwell's fierce expression tightened her gut.

"But they broke in my apartment." Connie wiped her cheeks and swallowed. "I'd left my address book open. I programmed Ellen's address into my GPS. I never thought to take it with me. It had all of your addresses on the open pages. Those pages are missing, torn out. Matt thinks they'll head up here."

A flurry of curses made the rounds. Connie felt horrible. "Maybe I should just leave. If I'm gone, there is no reason for them to come here."

"No. You'll be safe here." Ellen turned to Breccan and Max. "Won't she?"

"Yes," Kai spoke, hands tightening on her shoulders.

Max and Breccan shared a glance and nodded. "Of course."

Connie wasn't sure who spoke first, their voices

simultaneous. "Thank you."

"Mom, maybe you and Dad should stay here. I'd feel better." Ellen frowned.

"No, we'll stay home. It would be easy enough for them to see Connie isn't here. We should be fine."

"We'll make sure the local police know what's going on." Breccan whispered something to Max, who nodded.

"That sounds good. You all be safe. Connie, don't worry. If he comes around here, we'll catch him. We'll talk to you later, Ellen." A click and they were gone.

Kai put in a call to the local police, but found out Matt already called.

"Well, it looks like everyone has been contacted." Kai's eyes were faintly glowing, his face hard. "Now we need to make sure that no one can sneak in here."

"How are we going to do that?" Ellen asked. She looked worried. Breccan pulled her from her chair into his lap. Max moved behind them placing a hand on Ellen's shoulder.

Connie swallowed. Ellen's werewolves were still protective as ever. Thank goodness. Definitely a good thing, especially now. Breccan brought her attention back to the problem.

"We'll set up watches. One of us will stay with you both at all times." Breccan stated. "At night shouldn't be a problem." He nodded at Ellen. "You installed the alarm on the house when you moved in. Start using it again, along with the video system at the entrance to the drive."

"Good idea. I'll make sure the security cameras on the barns are activated too. That way we can see if anyone approaches that shouldn't be here. If the two of you stay close we should be able to protect you both." Both women started shaking their heads. Kai frowned. "What?"

"I work every day next week," Ellen answered. "Vacation coverage."

"I start my new job on Monday." Connie frowned. "Don't even think to stop me." Her stomach twisted. She needed this job, but was it going to be safe? She didn't want to bring danger to work.

All the men frowned.

Breccan spoke slowly. "Ellen, you should be okay

at work. We'll follow you up. Call when you are getting ready to leave and one of us will follow you home."

"That's ridiculous. I'll be fine at work. These people would have no way of finding me while I'm working." Ellen pouted. "I just finally started being able to do it on my own. How about if I call when I leave and I check in every few hours?"

"Make it every hour, and we'll meet you for lunch."

"I don't take a lunch break. I stop at the park for a few minutes, that's it."

"Then we'll meet you there." Maxwell nodded.

Ellen grimaced. "But…"

"That is non-negotiable. Call us so we have time to meet you," Maxwell said sternly.

He seemed to be the more serious one of the two, though Breccan had his moments from what Connie could see.

"I agree." Breccan tilted Ellen's head to look at him. "I don't intend to lose you. We just want you safe."

"Fine. I will." Both wolves look satisfied. Ellen snuggled back into Breccan.

"Connie, where are you working?" Kai scowled.

Connie rolled her eyes. "Remember, I said I got a job at the vet clinic."

"Yes, I do remember." His expression clearly exasperated. "But you never said where. There is more than one veterinarian in town."

"Oh. At the new one, Animal Kingdom."

"You should be okay at work." Kai grinned. "I thought I recognized the scent on you. I know the vet. He's my little brother." Connie looked stunned. Kai laughed at her expression. "I wasn't born under a rock. Dragons are rarely solitary creatures, despite the myths."

The men continued to make plans. Bored, Ellen showed Connie how to activate and deactivate the alarm. Connie started her clothes washing, anything to ignore the knot in her gut. She refused to show up to work in wrinkled scrubs. Thinking about work helped distract her.

"We're going to check out the system." Kai caressed her cheek. "Stay inside together until we have everything up and running."

"Fine." Connie hoped he didn't see the heat flush

her face. The most innocent touch sent a fire raging through her blood. She hadn't planned on anything more than hanging with Ellen anyway.

The door slammed shut behind the men. They had a plan.

Connie dropped her head to the table. "They are going to really be pains, aren't they Ellen?"

"You have no idea. But, Connie, at least they want us safe, it could be a lot worse." She flicked a finger at Ellen, stinging her ear.

"Ouch." Connie swatted away Ellen's hand without lifting her head. "How could it be worse?"

"They could be following us all day at work. Or they could forbid us to go."

"I'd like to see them try." Connie sat up, snorting.

"Connie, do you honestly think we could stop them?"

"I don't know." Connie exhaled shoving her chair back noisily. "Kai has no right to tell me what to do. I don't care what he says. How could I be his mate? Damn it, Ellen! I'm too young to settle down. I have too much I want to do."

Ellen laughed. Connie paced around the kitchen.

"Oh, so he told you. Connie, sit down. What is it you want to do? And remember I'm the same age as you."

"Phtt. You've always wanted to settle down, Ellen. You're so happy, it's crazy." Connie hugged Ellen before sitting. "And I'm happy for you. But I have a few years to go to be a veterinarian. I just finished undergraduate school. I'm going to veterinarian school in the fall. That's all I ever wanted, Ellen. I can't just give it up. I got in at U of I in Champagne-Urbana. It's a great school and cheaper since it's a state school. That's like at least a five-hour drive from here!"

"Connie." Ellen glowered. "Hold on a minute. What makes you think Kai would ask you to give it up?"

Connie looked at her and stilled. Ellen couldn't be right, could she? Would Kai be okay with her plans?

"But, he lives here."

"He could live anywhere, Connie."

"I want to travel when I finish my degree."

"Connie, did you really want to travel by yourself?"

"Uh. No. I always thought the two of us would go." Connie huffed and shook her head. "I always thought I'd be able to change your mind about travelling," she spoke slowly. "But you're getting married." She looked at Ellen, reality smacking her in the face. "There's no way you'd go now."

"No, there's not. And you know how hard it is for me now, going anywhere other than where I feel safe. Maybe I'd be able to by the time you graduate from veterinary school, but I don't want to. I've always wanted a home and family. But so did you." She grabbed Connie's hands. "Connie, there is nothing you said that should stop you from being with Kai. He's not bound here. You'd always be safe travelling with him. God, I can feel the chemistry between you two."

"I don't know, Ellen. I just don't feel ready yet. I thought..." Connie ran her hands through her hair, tugging on the ends.

"What? That love would come on your terms?" She shook her head. "Have you ever felt this way before? Are you willing to just give it up?"

Connie stood up and paced again, arms wrapped

around each other. "I can't think when he touches me, Ellen. I lose myself."

"Do you feel diminished? Do you really lose yourself, or are you finding stuff out about yourself you didn't know? Are you just scared?"

"Oh, all right!" Connie through her hands in the air. "It scares me, Ellen. He scares me. I never really thought about settling down. Kai makes me feel things I never thought I'd feel." Connie stopped. She could feel her stomach turning. "But Ellen, this is his home. The five hour one way trip would never work." She chortled. "Travelling with him might be fun though. But I'm not sure what I'd see other than the four walls of a hotel room!"

"Con, have you tried to get into UW?"

"No... Ellen, they have one of the top ten veterinarian schools in the US. I'm not sure I'd get in."

"Geez Connie! You carried a 4.0! They'd be lucky to have you. Maybe your new boss has some ties there and can put in a good word. What would it hurt to try?"

"Maybe. I have missed Wisconsin. How far is the drive to Madison from here?"

"It's about an hour." She looked at Connie hopefully. "Do you want to apply?"

It was quiet in the kitchen, Connie pacing thoughtfully while Ellen waited. It could work. The drive wasn't too bad. Part of her family lived here. Her heart quivered, and Kai was here. Breath catching, she stopped and nodded.

"I don't think I'd be happy if I gave him up, Ellen." Connie tugged her hair and glared at Ellen. "Don't you dare tell him! It just seems too fast. I've only known him a couple of days! I know I wouldn't be happy if I gave up being a vet, either. If I was able to get in at UW I could see him more often and get to know him better without rushing into anything." She nodded her head. That sounded reasonable. Too bad her body warred with her brain. Her hormones were all in with Kai's plan to mate. Stupid hormones. "Okay, Ellen, I'll try. I think it will be worth it. I'm pretty sure he's worth it, but I don't really know him, so I'd rather take it slow."

"That's great! It'll be so fun having you here."

"Ellen, wait a minute. I'll have to live near the campus. I have to take a full load. I'll need to be close to school to get my studying done and stuff. I won't be living here. I'll need some type of job to help support myself, too." Just thinking of it all, her stomach sank. She nibbled on a finger nail. A nasty habit she'd been trying to break.

"Oh. Well maybe the vet here would keep you on if you go to UW. Would that be enough do you think? You could stay here on weekends and work." Ellen's cheeks pinked with happiness. "Think of all the fun we could have."

"That would be perfect, actually. I could make sure I get all my studying done during the week, so most of my weekends would be free. That should work." She grinned happily at Ellen. "Providing, of course, that I can get into UW."

"Let's see what you have to do." Ellen got up. "We can check the application process out online."

Connie bit her lip. It was almost too much to hope for, but maybe it would work.

"All right, but Ellen, don't get your hopes up too high. The application time has probably passed. Especially for grad school."

"Well, that doesn't mean you can't try. I bet they have a waiting list or something. Don't forget, with your grades you'll definitely graduate, so their success rate would be higher."

Connie shook her head. "Ellen, where do you get this stuff?" She couldn't help the twinge of excitement thrumming through her. Maybe she could have everything she'd always wanted.

"Hey, I read. It's just common sense. The better the chances of graduation, the better the chance to have a larger group of Alumni, the better the chances of them bringing in more money. They need the money to run."

"Okay, okay! Let's go check their website." A bubble of happiness floated in her chest. Kai and her veterinarian degree. It couldn't get better than that, could it?

****

Dinner was a quiet affair. Ellen and Connie kept smiling at each other. Kai knew they must be up to some mischief, but decided not to press them.

"Did you solve the problem with the driveway camera?" he asked Breccan.

"Yes. A bird built its nest on it and blocked the sensor. It took a bit to clean it all up. Plus, I made sure the solar panel was clear. The base monitor is working. How are the cameras coming on the barn?" Breccan shoveled bites in his mouth between questions.

"Good. We have a few more to put up and then we can hook them into the system also. We should finish with no problem tomorrow." Kai nodded.

"Excellent. While I worked on the camera, one of the sheriff's deputies drove by. He stopped, curious as to what I was doing. I told him of the situation and our precautions. He'd already been apprised; the county sheriff is going to increase their patrols out our way. He said he'd let the sheriff know our precautions. They'd also make sure they responded right away if the alarm at the house went off."

"That means you have to make sure you set the alarm, ladies," Maxwell said. "I want it on at all times. If you leave, unlock it, and reset it. Same when you come in."

"Oh, for Pete's sake! That's going to be a pain. We're constantly in and out," Ellen griped.

"Then you can just stay in. That would work fine for me."

"Maxwell! I am not going to be stuck in the house." Ellen shook her head. "That's crazy."

"It's not. I am responsible for your safety and by extension, your cousin." Max growled. "You won't be stuck inside, however." He glanced at his brother. "Breccan already agreed if you weren't willing I couldn't force you. I'd feel better if you would." Max quirked an eyebrow at Ellen, frowning when she emphatically shook her head. "At least always have the alarm on when you're in the house. We'll all feel better if we know you're safe and no one has broken in."

She huffed. "Fine. What about the entrance from the barn? Is that alarmed too?"

"Yes. The tunnel is alarmed, from the bottom of the house and again at the entrances to the barn. You just have to reset each zone as you go through."

"When did the tunnel have alarms put in?"

"Your brothers were discussing it when they added

the house alarm. Breccan and I recommended it be added as a safety precaution. It wasn't enabled, but could be at the flick of a switch." The two grinned at each other, obviously proud of their foresight. Ellen rolled her eyes, while Connie laughed.

The rest of dinner talk was normal. Connie talked about the new job she was starting next week. Connie and Ellen went over wedding plans. Kai stared at Connie when he thought no one was looking. Her eyes sparkled with enthusiasm. Her golden hair calling to his dragon. She was his treasure, golden and shining. His dragon wanted to snatch her up and hide her from everyone. Kai clenched his hands. He couldn't do that, but he wanted to. Finally, dinner was done, and they all settled back in their chairs. Maybe he could get Connie alone again.

"Well, that was a nice dinner." He could hear the smile in Ellen's voice. "Why don't you guys have a seat on the porch and Connie and I'll clean up."

"Thanks for the dinner, Ellen. It was delicious." Kai inclined his head to Connie. "Both of you did a real nice job."

"I've a better idea. Who's up for a dip in the pond?

It's bound to be warm and it'll feel good in this heat." Breccan stood up. "Leave the dishes. We'll help you when we get back inside."

"That sounds good. What do you say, Ellen? I'll get my swimsuit." Connie headed toward her room. Kai took a step in her direction and then stopped. She hadn't invited him. His eyes followed her down the hall, watching the hypnotizing sway of her hips until she disappeared from sight.

"Sounds like fun. Maxwell, Kai, why don't you guys grab some beer and get some chairs set up out there?" Ellen turned to Breccan. "Help me with the dishes? Most of them are done, so I just have to scrape off the plates and put them in the dishwasher and turn it on."

"I can do that. Go get your suit on. Kai will be there." Breccan nudged her toward their room.

"I intended to. I don't want him seeing me naked. Hey, what about you? I don't want Connie seeing you either!"

Breccan gathered her in his arms. "We'll shift. What difference will it make?"

"Oh. I thought we'd play."

Breccan looked in her eyes and smiled.

"We can play as wolves. Or have you forgotten?" Breccan grinned as she blushed. He kissed her, hard. "Now, go get changed. Let me finish cleaning up." Ellen left him, still red as he chuckled.

"Kai, come on out. She's not going anywhere." Maxwell pressed his face against the screen.

Kai grumbled. The wolf was yanking at his tail.

Connie came out of her room and headed back toward the kitchen. Kai groaned. His groin tightened. He couldn't wait to get out of his jeans.

Connie wore a string bikini. A hot pink net cover draped across her body. It didn't really cover up much of anything. He swore he could see the outline of her aureoles, her nipples already at attention. She made him drool.

"Kai." Breccan nodded. "Let's go."

"Coming." He cleared his throat. "I'm coming."

"That's what I'm afraid of." Breccan chuckled. "I don't want to clean that up."

Kai snarled, shifting a fang out at Breccan. "Fine."

They headed to the porch. Kai couldn't look his fill, blocked by the house. The wolves nudged him down the stairs and partially across the yard. He could hear just fine though. The women's voices coming closer. Satisfied his mate would be back in his sight shortly, he headed toward the pond, trailing the two wolves.

"Connie, here's a towel." Kai could hear Ellen's voice. "Carry one for Kai, okay? I've got three here to carry."

"Sure, as long as he doesn't expect me to dry him off."

"Ya, sure, you don't wanna touch his body." Ellen snickered.

"You snot! Don't you dare say anything in front of him!" Kai heard the snap of a towel and Ellen came running out the door laughing.

"Breccan save me! Connie's being baaad." Connie ran after her, snapping her towel, both running toward the pond laughing.

Kai watched the young women burst out of the house. A smile gracing his face. They all heard the exchange. The wolves had excellent hearing. They knew

Connie was his. It was only a matter of time before he claimed her. Ellen ran into Breccan's arms grinning with joy. He closed his arms around her pulling her against his chest. Maxwell followed behind them. Ellen practically wiggled with happiness.

"Come on, let's go! I want to swim!" Ellen wriggled out of Breccan's arms. "Last one in is a rotten egg!"

Kai grabbed Connie around the waist as she ran by him. "Hey! Let me go!" He wrapped her in his arms, laughed, and released her. Connie looked at him and he could see a light blush painting her shoulders and face. She turned and ran toward the pond. "Wait for me, Ellen!"

The women ran to the pond, stripping off their cover ups. The men stripped down and shifted. With howls, growls and rumbles they took off after the women. Connie and Ellen looked back, screamed, laughed, and ran harder.

They dove into the pond, laughing and splashing, the three shifters gliding toward them. Well, he swum gracefully, the wolves on the other hand were doggie paddling. He snickered. They lazily circled the women; splashing back and watching them play. Breccan would brush up against Ellen, lifting her out and letting her slide back in the water. Maxwell finally joining in the fun. The wolves shifted, tossing Ellen back and forth, her screeches filled with laughter. Her laughter and the howling of the wolves echoed as they chased each other across to the other side of the pond. Kai figured it was a miracle they didn't drown as often as they flashed between human and wolf.

Kai watched Connie, seeing Ellen and her wolves play gave her a wistful look. Kai circled her, catching her attention, nudging her with his head. He was ever so much handsomer than the wolves. His scales gleamed in the low light. Connie giggled and pushed him away giving him a splash. Kai's eyes gleamed as he rumbled, glowing in the darkening evening. He glided around her rubbing against her, snorting warm air against her smooth belly. Her giggles set a throbbing down low in his abdomen. He was swift as an eel in the water. Connie backed up still smiling.

Kai dove under water and came up with Connie on

his back. She screeched and grabbed his neck. He dove again, taking her under with him, heading closer to the shore, on the opposite side from Ellen and her wolves. Kai changed as he did, twisting around to wrap his arms around Connie, trailing his hands up her legs, ass and back. Only her swimsuit impeded him. They rose to the surface, his arms filled, her sexy curves molded to his chest. Kai kissed Connie while pulling her tight against him, enjoying the heated depth of her mouth, the dueling of her tongue with his. The suddenness threw her off balance, eliminating any protest.

Connie wrapped her arms and legs around him, shivering. She arched against him, moaning, tightening her legs. Kai grew hard against her. Her warmth settling snuggly against his cock. The only thing separating them was her bikini. He wanted to rip it off and sink into her depths. Kai lowered his hands to cup Connie's bottom, moving her against him. Connie moaned, kissing him frantically. He kissed her deep and slow savoring the taste of her mouth while rocking against her. Connie tightened her arms around his neck.

CHAPTER SEVEN

Her sex softened preparing to take him in. Hot and urgent she never dreamed it could be this way. She couldn't seem to control herself. She wanted him in her now. Kai slid his hand over her cheek, slipping a finger in her bikini, stroking her slit. She squirmed, nipples pebbled, trying to take Kai's finger to stop the ache. Connie moaned, his finger penetrating her, teasingly, only to ease out and circle her, dipping in and out as his other hand kneaded her bottom. She ached.

Connie moaned, rubbing against Kai's cock as his fingers spread her, shifting his cock to stroke against her. His touch scalding and she realized her bikini bottom was no longer covering the essentials. Her heart raced. She could feel his hardness, the silky skin of his shaft causing her womb to clench.

He thrust against her, the head of his cock rubbing her clit, his cock sliding between her lips, but not penetrating, like riding a pole. Frantically, Connie bit his neck, her teeth worrying his skin, desperate to feel him fill her. Manly musk and salt burst on her taste buds. She wanted more.

Kai thrust harder against her, penetrating her with his fingers. Connie sobbed, moving against Kai, arching to fuck his fingers and ride as much of his cock as he let her. She shook, Kai's mouth covering her scream. She rode his hand harder, wanting his cock inside her. Suddenly, he pulled his fingers out and penetrated her. Connie cried out against his mouth, convulsing as he rammed into her. Starbursts lit her eyelids and she realized they were closed, her body desperate for his touch. Her pussy throbbed as it stretched to accommodate him. She tightened her arms and legs around him, frantically riding him, the pull and slide of his thickness making her crazy with want. She wailed, face against his neck as he rubbed a finger against her clit as he fucked her faster and faster. She bucked and bit his neck again. Kai grew harder and began pulsing inside of her, coating her womb with warmth. Connie wailed her pleasure, muffling herself against his neck. He pulsed inside her. Her body shook, milking Kai.

"Oh, my God," Connie said softly. "Oh." She lifted her head only to drop back against his shoulder. "Oh, my god! I can't believe we just did that!" She tried to push away, wriggling, but Kai held tight, still penetrating her. She shuddered, nipples peaking. He felt so good. But this was crazy. "Let me go! God, Ellen and the guys are here! Kai, please! Let me go! I don't do this! What are they going to think of me? Oh God, we didn't even use a condom!" Connie struggled trying to wiggle away. Each wiggle caused him to lengthen again inside her. How could she resist him?

"Connie." She wasn't paying any attention to him. Her thoughts swirled in her head. "Connie." Kai grasped her face with one hand, his arm around her waist. "Connie, look at me." His voice was sharp. She looked at him, but all she could think of was the hot, thick dick inside her. She couldn't concentrate, just panic. It felt too good. "It's dark. Ellen and her mate are on the other side of the pond. They don't even know." He rocked her against him. She looked at him, her big blue eyes rimmed with tears. He groaned and kissed her softly. "It's okay."

Kai bucked into her, his girth stretching her, sending shards of pleasure through her body. Each thrust and she shivered, tightening on him, aftershocks shaking her body. Kai stiffened with each grasp of her body, slowing down to a smooth glide. Kai groaned and kissed her, ravaging her mouth. He held her tight and ground against her. Connie moaned in surrender. He could do as he wished. She was putty in his arms. It was too much, but never enough.

Kai pumped faster and faster forcing her to ride him as he fucked her. She convulsed against him, a thin wail escaping as she rode him. He pulled her tight, his hands bruising in their force as he came, shooting into her womb. Connie rubbed against him, shaking as she continued down from the high she got from riding Kai. They floated, both seemingly content. He pulled from her softness, groaning as he slid from her tight sheath. The feeling sending ripples of desire through her.

Connie moaned and shivered. The feel of him pulling loose left her with a sense of loss. She dropped her head on his shoulder, arms tightening around his shoulders. "Are you sure it's okay?" She tightened her hold around him. He reached down, his fingers lingering, teasing her clit and tracing her slit before adjusting her suit back in place. Mmm, those fingers were just as talented as the rest of him.

"I'm sure. They're making enough noise they wouldn't have even heard us." Connie tilted her head. She could hear Ellen's laughter, a man's laughter and growling amidst lots of splashing.

She sniffled and giggled through her tears. "That's not what I meant! Though it sounds like there're ten people over there instead of three!"

"So, are you okay now?" Kai inquired. She nodded and snuggled against him. "Ready to get out?" His voice lowered, the sound bringing comfort to her soul.

"No." She burrowed closer to his neck. "Can you just hold me?" Kai's arms tightened. She felt more vulnerable than this morning. Her tears trailed against his shoulder. She wasn't even sure why she cried. "I don't do this kind of thing! I just met you."

"It's okay." He kept his arms around her, running one hand up and down her back. "It's natural between mates."

Connie stilled against him. "Quit saying that." She reared back with a frown on her face. "I just met you and you're too bossy to live with. No way can I be your mate!"

Kai chuckled, low and deep. Connie could feel it reach inside her. She pushed away from him, swimming backwards and muttering. She would not, could not admit, how hard pulling away from him felt. She turned and then headed toward Ellen. Suddenly, she stopped, whipping around to face him again.

"What's the matter?"

"Kai. We didn't use any birth control." Connie looked at him. "I'm not ready to be a mother."

His eyes glowed. "Does that mean one day you will?"

"Kai." Connie glared. "That's not the point."

He flashed a grin. "Don't worry. You can't get pregnant right now. You're not in heat."

"What? Did you say 'in heat'? I'm not an animal."
She ground her teeth. He tempted her to just take a bite
out of him, and not in a fun way.

"Until we are mated you won't get pregnant,
Connie. Nor do I carry any diseases." He laughed. "I've
had all my shots."

She rolled her eyes and chuckled. "Distemper
too?"

"Funny girl." He started swimming toward her, a
determined look in his eye. She turned and started
swimming away as fast as she could. "You can run,
Connie. For now." Kai ducked under the water. Connie
knew he shifted, his tail flicking out of the water headed
in her direction. A twist of excitement coiled in her belly.
She got closer to Ellen. He surfaced behind her, lifting
Connie up, so she slid down his side. She shrieked and
laughed dropping into the water. Kai swam around her,
gracefully sliding around her. Bumping her with his head
and rubbing against her.

The sounds of their laughter, the rumbles and
howls of the shifters spread across the fields as darkness
settled in for the night. No one noticed the watcher in the

woods.

****

Connie stepped out on the porch, coffee in hand. The house seemed to be deserted this morning, or Ellen was sleeping in. She yawned, looking at her watch. Well, maybe she was just early. It was just after dawn. The darn rooster woke her up. Connie thought roosters crowing at dawn just a myth. Evidently, no one passed the message on to Ellen's. No matter how she tried to get back to sleep it didn't work. She glanced up and there was Kai, watching her, eyebrow raised. Confused, Connie glanced at him. She wasn't sure what he was gesturing.

Shaking his head, Kai headed toward her. "What did we tell you? You have to set the alarm when you leave."

"Oh! I forgot." She smiled sheepishly at him. "It's early."

Kai tapped her on the chin. "It's to keep you safe. Did you deactivate it when you came outside?" Her eyes widened. Oops, she forgot. Glancing up at Kai, she shook her head. He cursed and strode into the house. He entered a deactivation code and whipped out his cell phone. "This is Kai Ignis. Our code wasn't deactivated and I wanted to let you know it's a false alarm. Don't worry about sending out a deputy." He nodded and sighed. "Mm hm. Okay. That's fine. We'll be expecting them. Thanks." He could hear a siren getting closer. Soon even Connie would be able to hear it.

"What?"

"They want to see how fast the response time is, so the deputy is on his way."

"Oh." Connie nibbled her lip. "Am I in trouble? I really did forget."

"Not from the sheriff's department. It's me you have to worry about." Connie blinked up at him, big blue eyes wide. She fluttered them, just a bit. "Don't give me that look. This is for your safety."

She hung her head, peeking up at him through her lashes, a pout on her lips. "I know. I just forgot. It seems so peaceful here. I have a hard time even thinking there could be trouble."

"There can be trouble anywhere. If you don't start remembering, there will be trouble, and it will be from me." He looked down into her eyes, his determined look showing her he meant business. "Do not forget again, Connie. This will be the last time I warn you."

Connie glared at him. She knew it was necessary to do what he said for her and Ellen's safety. But she really hated when he got bossy. "Fine. I just forgot. It won't happen again." She knew he could hear the aggravation in her voice. She knew because he grinned down at her as she spoke and it drove her crazy.

He flicked a finger off her nose and smiled at her. She growled. He only laughed and leaned down to give her a quick kiss and a stinging smack on her ass.

"Oh!" She couldn't stop the quick exclamation, he'd surprised her. She rubbed her butt. Connie couldn't believe he'd done that.

"Remember." Kai turned away laughing and headed to the squad car that came careening down the drive to stop in a billow of dirt by the barn.

Connie stuck out her tongue and flounced into the house. *Who does he think he is, anyway?* She shut the door and stomped into the kitchen. Looking out the window at Kai and seeing him frown, she ignored him and refilled her coffee. Overbearing dragon! Remembering the alarm, she headed over to set it. No reason to give him more ammunition.

She'd just wanted to relax and sit in the swing to drink her coffee, soak in a bit of sun. Pouting, Connie sat at the table. Shaking her head, a smile creeping across her face at her childlike actions, she laughed.

"That man is driving me crazy," she whispered to herself.

"They will do that." Ellen stood in the door grinning at her.

Connie started, lifted her head and shrugged.

"I know. Try having two of them bossing you around." Ellen sniffed the air. "God, coffee. I hope there's some left." Ellen headed over and grabbed a cup, filled it, and drew a deep breath over the steaming liquid.

"You're starting to act like the rest of them. Sniffing everything."

Ellen laughed. "How can you not love the smell of coffee? I think I've always sniffed it."

Connie smiled and nodded. She loved the aroma. "True. I think I do it too. There's nothing better than that first cup in the morning."

"I'm willing to prove you wrong." The deep baritone thrilled her to her toes.

Connie turned and spun to the door behind her, a small scream escaping her lips.

Kai stood there grinning.

"How did you get in here? I didn't even hear the door open!" Connie added. She felt flustered. Not just from his sneaky ways, but because just looking at him caused her heart to flutter.

"I came in through the door. Right behind you." Kai gave her a stern look that made her squirm. "Anyone coming through here would have snatched you in an instant." He leaned down and stared into her face. "So, remember the alarm."

Connie sniffed. So rude. "I told you I just forgot. I remembered to set it when I came back in."

"No, you didn't. I saw you in the kitchen and then head back over to set it."

Connie glared. "But I remembered."

"Don't forget again."

"And what if I do?" *Jerk.* Connie pushed back her chair and stood up, glaring at him, hands fisted on her hips. "What are you going to do about it?"

Kai tossed her over his shoulder and strode toward her room.

Connie shrieked, pounding on his shoulder. "Let me down!"

"I'll show you what I'll do about it." The rumble in his chest and his actions sent shivers through Connie. Ellen's laughter following them didn't help. Connie thought maybe, just maybe she shouldn't have poked the dragon.

****

Kai headed toward Connie's bedroom. Her pouts and defiance stirred his dragon sending him into an uproar. He was determined to make his mate behave. All he wanted was to keep her safe. Well, and to strip her naked and sink in deep.

Her squirming and muttering over his shoulder

hardened his cock even more. Hell, just seeing her on the porch in that itty, bitty nightgown made him hard. He thought he'd burst his jeans. When she pouted all he could think of was her lips wrapped around his cock, licking and sucking him. She may not be experienced, but he'd teach her exactly what he liked. Starting now.

Kai kicked her door wider, and slammed it behind him. Connie seemed to understand his seriousness. *Good*, he thought, *about time*.

Striding over to her bed, he stripped off the comforter, already in a jumble and tossed it to the floor. He slid Connie down and sat at the end of the bed, holding her in front of him.

"I'm going to make sure you don't forget again. Nothing will happen to you, do you understand?"

Connie's over dramatized sigh and "Fine, whatever," aggravated him. Kai grabbed her and pulled her over his lap. He flung up her nightgown and froze. His gut clenched. She wore on another thong, this one a hot pink.

Growling, he pulled them off, one hand on her back holding her down as she squirmed.

"Stop it! What do you think you're doing?" she shrieked. "Ellen, help me!"

Kai could hear Ellen laughing in the kitchen, interspersed with deeper chuckles. He smiled in satisfaction. No help would be coming for Connie.

Looking at the ivory globes of her ass, Kai caught flashes of her pussy as she tried to get away from him. Her struggles called to the dragon in him, rising to the surface and wanting nothing more than to devour her. But first, she would learn to listen. Kai grabbed her nightgown and stripped it off.

She lay like a sacrifice of old. Unable to get away, but struggling all the same. Her ivory skin begged to be caressed. The weight of her breasts against his leg exciting him. His eyes sharpened and he could scent her arousal, along with a dose of fear. Good. She needed to learn to listen for her own safety. And his sanity. If he lost her, Kai didn't know what it would do to him.

His grin was sharp and predatory. Luckily, Connie couldn't see it. He held her, enjoying her halfhearted struggle. Kai kept one hand on her at all times. He didn't want her to think she could get away, and reached down and caressed her breasts. He grinned, his erection even harder at the feel of her soft skin. Her nipples hard from excitement. He plucked them, making her squirm even more.

"Ohhh!" Her voice was half grumpy, half excited. Kai laughed, playing with her nipples as the scent of her arousal increased. He needed to check.

Changing hands, keeping her across his lap, he slid a finger through her wetness, sinking into her sopping passage. His thumb lightly rubbing her clit. Connie moaned and arched into his hand. Her body begging for more. Kai grinned. Thrusting in and out until she was close to her peak, Kai removed his hand and licked his fingers. Her honey tasted decadent.

"More." Her moan low and grudgingly given as she arched up searching for satisfaction.

"Not yet. I'm going to make sure you remember to set the alarm and lock the door." With that, Kai brought his hand down on her cheek. Connie screamed. Struggling to get away, Kai held her down spanking her, alternating between cheeks. When he was done, Connie was moaning and her ass flushed pink. He loved the sight, a rosy blush against her pale skin.

Kai rubbed her ass, chuckling as she followed his hand. He slid a hand down and speared her again. He smiled in satisfaction. Even wetter than before. Kai thrust in and out of her, gradually introducing a second finger.

Connie moaned and squirmed upon his intrusion.

Kai continued, finding and hitting the spot making his mate scream out in satisfaction. His dragon gloated inside. He loved the scent and sight of her draped across him. She squeezed his fingers, humming as he slowed and stopped. Pulling his fingers out, he slid them in his mouth, licking her juices off his hand. Ambrosia.

"Oh, my." Connie lay sprawled across his lap, no longer trying to get away. Her whisper sent him chuckling. Kai manhandled her, spinning her to sit in his lap. Her body a warm bundle laying boneless in his arms.

He loved her look. Her eyes were soft, confusion and satiation evident in her gaze. Her skin was flushed pink, nipples hard, and her sex dark pink and glistening as she curled into his chest and arms. Kai could feel a rumble build in his chest. *Mine.*

He held her to him, not wanting to let her go. His

treasure. Connie stirred in his arms, her butt wiggling against his erection. He held her tighter, making sure she didn't fall. A giggle drifted to his ears.

"Was the spanking supposed to make me remember to lock and arm the door?" She whispered, sounding way too happy.

"Yes."

"Does that mean you'll only do it if I'm bad?" She giggled. "I might have to be bad on purpose."

Kai frowned. "Next time, you won't enjoy it. It will be a punishment. This was a warning."

"Pfft."

A sharp slap on her ass had Connie squeaking. "Ow!"

"Behave, woman." He frowned at her but knew he couldn't disguise the twinkle in his eye. Her fluttering lashes, as she peeked at him while suppressing a grin, showed him that. "Don't forget or you won't enjoy the next spanking."

He spread his legs and dropped her to her knees in front of him. Her arms curved along his thighs and she tucked her fingers into his belt.

"Did you want something?" Connie flirted up at him, lashes fluttering as she batted her eyes at him. She ran a finger along his belt, playing with the buckle. She giggled when he grunted and ran a finger along his zipper. "Does this hurt?"

Kai grabbed her hand. The little tease enjoying this. He could see her youth in how she played, uninhibited yet shy, as evidenced by the flush of pink rising from her breasts to tint her cheeks. Pulling her hands away, he unbuckled his belt and spread his pants. His throbbing cock sprang out, pointing straight toward her. He wanted her mouth on him. Ached to feel her tongue lick and suck him deep into her throat.

He heard her breath catch and watched her nipples tightening. Kai lifted up and pulled his jeans down. Connie grabbed them and pulled them to the floor. They wouldn't come off, his boots were in the way.

Kai caught his breath. Before he could take them off, Connie engulfed him into her mouth. The hot moistness of her throat, her suckling him, made him groan. Grabbing her head, Kai thrust in, pumping in and out. The sight of her pouty lips surrounding him sent heat twisting to his abdomen. His cock growing harder, longer. His balls tightened, pleasure spiraling up his spine.

"Mmm." The vibration of her throat made him groan. Pulling her hair and tilting her head back, he held her captive speeding up his thrusts. Connie choked and Kai froze. He tried pulling out, aching and desperate but she sucked him back in. Back into her tight hot throat. Damn.

"Are you okay?" He swallowed hoarsely. He tried not to move, waiting on her answer. She nodded, still suckling him. He groaned when she took his balls in her hands and stroked them. Desperately needing to move, but afraid he'd blow, Kai pulled her off and up, unable to stand the torture any longer. He almost blew as she held on, only coming free with a pop as he dragged her up, breasts bouncing in reaction, drawing his eye and making his mouth water.

"Hey! I wasn't done." Her pout almost made him lose control. Those lips were made to surround his cock.

"Neither am I," Kai growled.

He pulled her to him, settling her so she straddled

him and thrust up, groaning, surrounded by her heat. Grabbing her hips, Kai controlled her, raising and lowering her while he pumped madly. Her body tried to hold him in with each stroke, her tightness squeezing him. Kai thrust up and held her down as he exploded inside her, jetting streams of seed. Connie cried out, her passage clinging. She quivered, shattering on top of him. She exhaled, falling limply against his chest.

"You're going to kill me," she whispered.

Kai chuckled. "But what a way to go." He lay back, moving so her legs straddled his. He was still snuggly ensconced inside her warmth and he planned to stay there for a while. Maybe even for round two.

CHAPTER EIGHT

Connie woke up slowly, her body aching, but in a good way. Her lady parts ached. It felt like they took a pounding. Stretching, giggling, she guessed they had. She didn't have any idea how to resist Kai. Not that she really wanted to anyway.

She rolled over. Where was he, anyhow? She remembered falling asleep on top of him, his dick still tucked inside her, radiating heat that seemed to flow through her body. Even after he'd blown inside her, he still felt hard. It must be because he was a dragon.

She couldn't remember him leaving. Connie felt empty without him inside her. She clenched, wanting to feel him. All she felt was emptiness. She whimpered. Kai was addictive.

Sitting up, she saw her nightgown folded on the end of her bed. Looking around she didn't see her panties. Standing up, she pulled the cover over the bed. Pulling clothes out of the dresser, Connie laid them on the bed and headed toward the shower.

She stopped as she looked into the trash can and grimaced. Connie knew Kai took her panties off without ripping them, but there they were, in the trash. She leaned over to pull them out and laughed. He must have torn them later. She tossed the ripped panties back in the trash. She'd have to get even with him. She wasn't going to start going commando, especially at work. He was just going to have to live with the fact she wore them.

Connie smiled as she thought about how she could pound that fact into his head. She brushed her teeth, again. She hated to take away the taste of Kai, but after having coffee and sleeping she felt the fuzzies and needed her mouth clean again. Rinsing, she turned on the shower to let it warm up.

Steam billowed in the room, taking a deep breath,

the damp warmth filled her lungs. Stepping into the shower and tipping back her head, Connie let the water run down her face and along her body. She groaned, relaxing in the heat. The warm water eased her muscles flowing along her skin. Getting thoroughly wet, she quickly scrubbed down. Closing her eyes, Connie rinsed, standing in the spray as the soap ran off her.

"You're gorgeous."

The rough voice startled her, making her squeak. His chuckle ticked her off a bit. Connie narrowed her eyes, turning toward him. Looking at Kai, she couldn't stay annoyed. He leaned against the vanity, arms crossed admiring her. Connie knew he liked what he saw. The proof was in his pants.

"Like what you see?" It came out on a whisper and giggle. She acted like a teenager with her first crush and couldn't seem to stop. She could feel her nipples harden. Her lady parts, more slut parts, around him, went hot and wet.

"Very, very much." He adjusted himself in his pants, no embarrassment at all. "Look what you do to me."

Connie's cheeks bloomed with heat. She couldn't help it. She could try to be a vamp, but no matter how hard she tried, the heat rose in her cheeks. She craved him and couldn't decide whether she should be embarrassed or grab him. Her fingers itched to do just that.

"Why are you in my bathroom?" She leaned over to grab a towel, but he beat her to it. Connie grabbed the other and quickly leaned over and stood, wrapping her hair. She giggled. The look on his face was priceless.

"How do you do that?" He shook his head. "Never mind, I came here to wake you for lunch and since you were in the shower I figured I could dry you."

"I can dry myself."

"I know. I just want to do it." Kai's eyes were hot. There was no way to resist that look. His glance sent heat streaking through her. Maybe he needed just a bit of a tease. She lifted a leg and stepped slowly out of the shower. She stood facing him, surrendering to her need to be touched.

Kai started rubbing her down, making sure each crack and crevice was dry. He wrapped the towel around her and pulled her against him. The feel of his heat radiating through the cotton of his shirt, her breasts aching and making her squirm against him.

"Hungry?"

His deep voice reverberated inside her. Her loins clenched, wanting him. She just couldn't keep giving in. Gathering her self-respect and what little control she had left, Connie stepped back, firmly tucking in the ends of the towel. She was surprised Kai let her. She knew in a battle of strength, he'd win.

"If lunch is done, I need to get dressed." Connie spun and headed quickly to the bedroom. Kai's low chuckle irked her. Looking at what she laid out, she changed her mind. Two could play at that game. Grabbing a short flouncy sundress from the closet, she dropped it on the bed. She debated, the pink sun dress or the short shorts and tank top?

"I thought you were getting dressed?"

"I'm not sure what I want to wear." Connie didn't bother to look up. She could practically hear his eyes roll.

"I thought you had clothes set out. They were on the bed when I came in."

"I don't know if I want to wear them."

"They're just clothes."

"Whatever. Go to lunch and I'll be right there."

Connie couldn't help the moan when Kai's lips slid against her neck. She tilted her head, giving him greater access. She shivered when he scraped his teeth at the tender joint of her neck and shoulder.

"Don't be too long." Kai stood almost touching her. She could feel the heat radiating from his body. "You could wear the dress, no underwear. That way I can touch you."

Connie shuddered, just the thought making her damp. A final kiss and he left, closing the door silently behind him. She exhaled, firming her shoulders. Two could play at that game.

"Dammit." She intended on wearing the dress to tease him. Somehow she knew she would be the one sorry. Grabbing the shorts and tank, she made sure she put on underwear. Too bad she didn't have any granny panties like her mom wore. She giggled at the thought of Kai's expression if he saw them on her. The tank was white, so she made sure her bra was hot pink. He couldn't help but notice.

Tossing the towel over the bathroom vanity and quickly making her bed, Connie stepped out of the room and headed to lunch, a teasing wiggle with each step closer to Kai. This would be fun.

****

Kai held his smile in as Connie sauntered into the room. He'd been afraid she'd wear that flirty little number. Knowing her, she'd have gone bare underneath just to tease him. Kai would have killed any man on the farm that looked at her. One strong wind and she'd have been showing the world her assets. His assets. He didn't share.

Luckily, he'd seen her grab it from the closet and made sure she wouldn't wear it. At least, that's what he'd hoped. Thank goodness telling her that she'd be more accessible to him changed her mind. She was a contradiction of bold and hesitancy. She'd make a magnificent dragon.

"Hey, sleepyhead. I just made hoagies," Ellen

called out.

Kai reached out an arm and pulled Connie onto his lap before she could sit.

"No dress? But I wanted to play." Kai felt her shudder in his arms at his whisper. He ran a finger across the neckline of the tank tap, watching the goose bumps form on her cleavage as his finger traced the exposed curves of her breasts. He chuckled as she flushed and struggled to get up.

"Let me up. I'm hungry." Kai let her up with a pat on her butt, earning him a glare from Connie and a laugh from Ellen. "Where are Breccan and Maxwell?"

"They're on their way in." Ellen leaned out the window to check. "Did you want anything to drink?"

Connie walked over to the counter. "I can get it. I'll just grab some milk. How about you? You already made lunch."

"No problem. Grab me a glass, too. Kai you want anything to drink?"

"I'll just have water."

"Connie, grab that for him, will you?"

"Sure. I don't mind waiting on him, when he's

perfectly capable of doing it himself. I live to serve." She stuck her tongue out at him.

"Don't be a pain." Ellen shook her head, smiling, and grabbed plates from the cabinet.

Kai just smiled. He'd have her serve him all right. His thoughts were interrupted by the arrival of Breccan and Maxwell. Maxwell took his position as beta seriously. He always appeared to be on guard. A good thing, especially now that Connie and Ellen needed protection. They couldn't let their guard down until the criminals were caught. Kai just hoped whatever trouble Maxwell prepared for stayed away.

"Afternoon, Kai." Breccan nodded at him. "Or should I say morning?" His grin mischievous. "We haven't seen too much of you so far today."

Connie blushed at the comment. Kai chuckled.

"That's because I had other business to attend to."

"Mm hm. I'm sure you did." Breccan waggled his brows up and down. "I'm sure you did."

Maxwell laughed. Kai shook his head. The two wolves had quite a comedy routine going, or so they thought.

"Are the cameras all ready to go?" Kai ignored their teasing. They needed to be serious. His mate's safety depended on it.

Breccan sobered. "Yes. You just need to patch them into the main board, so we can test them."

"Good. After lunch I'll get that done. I want to make sure the whole perimeter of the house is covered. I don't want any blind spots. We'll work together to make sure it's all covered."

They nodded. Kai knew neither of them wanted Ellen endangered in any way. She didn't do well with strangers. They would take no chances. It was one of the reasons they didn't give away they were shifters. They were afraid that as men Ellen would reject them. They needed her to trust them as wolves first. Kai knew what they were from the first and confronted them. Once he knew they weren't about to hurt Ellen, he stepped back.

The talk continued to be about security around the farm. Ellen and Connie were talking wedding dresses and shopping in town. Kai wasn't thrilled. One of the men would have to go with and he wasn't about to leave Connie's safety to the wolves.

Sandwiches done, the girls cleaned up the plates. Kai kicked back and watched. He could see Connie peeking at him when she thought he wasn't looking. His heart filled, a deep seated joy expanding his chest. Connie could say all she wanted about not believing in the 'mate stuff,' but she was as drawn to him as he to her.

Kai knew she was his mate, his treasure. He would prove it to her. He smirked, his gut tightening. He would enjoy that.

Leaning against the counter, Connie chatted and laughed with Ellen. The sound of their laughter brought a smile to his face. Leaning back, her lithe body relaxed, he couldn't help but drink her in. Her slightly messy pony tail, the skin tight white tank with the pink bra showcasing her plump breasts had his mouth watering. She turned and his eyes followed the line of her back, stopping momentarily on her rear end. Her cutoffs were cut short, hinting at the curve of her cheeks. Damn. He'd bet she wore one of those sexy thongs he'd seen strewn around her room.

Kai wanted nothing more than to carry her to her room and ravish her. She'd argue and fuss, but once his hands were on her she'd melt. He pulled back from his lascivious thoughts when the girls turned, heading out of the kitchen.

Kai reached out and pulled Connie to him, settling her in his lap before she escaped. He held on as she squirmed to get away, enjoying her soft body with each wiggle.

"Where are you heading off to?" He ran his lips along her neck, teasing goose bumps and shivers from her. Satisfaction curled in his gut. Only a matter of time and she would be his.

"We're going dress shopping. Ellen said one of the stores in town carries wedding and bridesmaid's dresses."

"Who is going with? Breccan or Maxwell?"

"Neither! Breccan can't see Ellen in her wedding dress."

"Why not?" He couldn't resist another nibble of her delectable neck.

"Because he can't." She sounded a bit aggravated. "Breccan can't see her in her dress until she walks down the aisle."

"Why?"

"It's bad luck." She tugged at his arms trying to get up. "Stop it. Let me up. We need to get going, so we have time to look."

"You can't go without one of us. Maxwell can go." Kai swore she growled, but Connie didn't say anything. He held in a chuckle, her bottom lip slowly making itself known in a pout. He could practically hear her brain whirl. The lip, the small frown that appeared between her eyes. "Or I can go with you," Kai added slowly. He made sure he held in his laugh at her expression. Her attempted manipulation amused him. He'd planned on going. Connie didn't need to know that.

Connie raised her eyes, peeking at him through her lashes. "Really? I thought you needed to check out the cameras."

"I do. Can you wait half an hour? It shouldn't take me long." He looked at her, putting on a stern face. "It is important for your safety." And his peace of mind.

Ellen stuck her head in the kitchen before Connie answered. "Sure we can. I wanted to change anyhow. It will be easier to try stuff on if I only have to change from a dress. You might want to change too, Connie."

Kai groaned. Connie giggled at the noise. "I guess I'll wear the sundress after all." Kai buried his face in her neck, loving the fresh clean scent rising from her skin.

"Go, while I can still keep my hands off of you. I'll be back as soon as the cameras are done." Kai grabbed her waist and stood her up. Spinning her and slapping her on the ass. "Go get changed."

She whirled, her mercurial temperament evident as she glared at him. "Don't do that." Then she turned and stomped out to his laughter.

CHAPTER NINE

Connie couldn't believe him. If he slapped her behind one more time she would…she didn't know what she'd do, but he'd be sorry. She shook her head, biting her lip. He made her hot and he did it to get her riled up. The more time she spent with him, the more she felt the pull. She headed into her bedroom and sat, head in her hands, tugging on her hair.

Connie didn't know what to do. Like she told Ellen, she didn't think she'd be able to walk away from Kai. He was everything she wanted in a man, or so he seemed, but it was too fast. She wanted to finish school. She'd dreamed of being a veterinarian. All she could do was hope she got in the UW program. Then maybe she could have both.

Checking the time, Connie jumped up and changed. Ellen was right, it would be easier to change from a dress rather than her shorts and tank. She checked in the closet with a grin. She would have fun flirting with Kai. Pulling out the dress she'd planned on wearing earlier. She giggled and changed into a barely there thong. Let him wonder what she was wearing under her skirt. She figured she better wear a heel too. Grabbing her makeup bag, she headed to the bathroom and quickly swiped some mascara and lip gloss on. She carried the heeled sandals, headed into the kitchen and dropped them by the door. Ellen and Kai were nowhere around.

"Ellen, are you almost ready?" Connie yelled.

"Yes," Ellen hollered back. "I'll be out in a minute."

Connie sat at the table and waited. Her mind shifting back to Kai. He brought back her dreams of a husband and family. Besides having their weddings practically planned, Ellen and she wanted lots of kids, both swearing at least half a dozen. Growing up changed those dreams, but Kai was bringing them back. The thought of a little dark haired boy, eyes sparkling as he chased his sister around the farm warmed her heart.

Half a dozen kids, Connie chuckled. She must have been crazy. No way could she afford six kids, not to mention the toll it would take on her body. Not that she couldn't stay in shape, she supposed.

She cocked her head. Someone retched. It was just Ellen and her in the house. Getting up, she headed toward Ellen's room. She pushed open the door, peering into the room. Ellen wobbled out of her bathroom. She looked pale.

"Ellen, what's the matter? We don't have to go today, you know." Connie moved, wrapping her arms around her. Ellen looked fine a little while ago. Now, pale and shaky looking, Connie urged her toward the bed, "Sit down, you look like you're going to fall down."

"I feel like shit." Ellen plopped down on the end of the bed and dropped back, keeping her arms wrapped around her middle.

"You look like it. What's wrong?"

"I think I'm coming down with a tummy bug." She

rolled toward Connie. "Can you get me my phone? I want to see if the doctor can get me in." She gave a ghost of a smile. "If Breccan finds out, he'll have me there before I can blink an eye, so I might as well beat him to it."

Connie looked around the room, and spying it on the dresser, brought it over. "Well, if he can't see you today, we'll stay home. You can take a nap and I'll look over the internet for ideas. Check Pinterest. There's lots of ideas there."

Ellen gave a low chuckle. "You'll be on there for hours."

Connie shrugged and grinned. "So?" She nodded at the phone. "Call your doctor and find out."

Connie sat on the bed while Ellen dialed and spoke. Ellen's room was huge. Decorated in shades of blue, brown and green, soothing. She imagined she sat in the center of a peaceful glade under a cloudless sky.

Ellen hung up and groaned. "Well, let's get ready. He can see me in forty-five minutes."

"Do you need any help?"

"No. I'm dressed, but I'm not sure we'll see any

dresses today."

Connie rolled her eyes. "Not my main concern if you're not feeling well." She stood up. "C'mon, let's get going. Did you brush your teeth?"

"Yes, and rinsed my mouth." Ellen made a face. "It tasted too nasty not to." She stretched out her hands. "Help me up."

"Okay, well, we've been at least half an hour. Kai should be ready." Connie reached out her hands and pulled. Ellen smacked into her as she stood and both started giggling. "Ow!"

"Well, move back, jeez." Ellen spoke through her giggles. "I want a glass of ginger ale before I go. I'm sure they'll make me pee in a cup or something." They headed to the kitchen.

"Sit at the table, I'll pour you a glass." Connie grabbed a glass and the soda from the refrigerator. Pouring a cup, she handed it to Ellen. "Here you go." She put the bottle back in the refrigerator.

The door opened and Kai stuck his head in. Yup, still hot. Connie's panties dampened. Darn it. Ellen needed her. She didn't have time to drool over Kai, even if she multitasked.

"Are you two ready to go?"

"In a minute. Soon as Ellen's done. She was thirsty." Connie pushed the refrigerator door shut. Oops, she'd already done that. Just checking, yeah, it wasn't like Kai's presence rattled her. No siree.

"That's fine. I need to wash up." Kai headed to the sink, brushing by Connie and running a hand along her jaw. A tingle ran from her jaw all the way down to her toes.

Ellen stood and placed the glass by the sink. "I'm ready." She went to the door and slipped on her sandals.

Connie followed and put on her flip flops. They probably wouldn't get to the dress store. Kai dried off and ushered the two of them out of the house, setting the alarm.

"I've already pulled the truck up." He opened the door and turned, lifting Connie up by the waist and setting her on the seat.

His hands, so firm against her waist lingered, sending butterflies attacking her middle. He finally let go. She scooted to the center, taking a deep breath.

"You next, Ellen." Kai grabbed Ellen's hand and helped her in. Shutting the door firmly behind her. He rounded the cab to climb in.

"I didn't know they still made bench seats." Connie smoothed her hands on either side caressing the leather.

"It's practical." He started the truck and pulled down the drive, going slowly.

Ellen clicked her belt in. "Yes. I checked a few places to find it. This is mine, or rather the banks, while I pay it off." Ellen's color looked better.

Connie grabbed her hand and squeezed. "Feeling better?"

"Yes, thanks." Ellen nodded. "Kai, I need to stop at the clinic on the way."

"Why? Breccan didn't say anything. He or Maxwell would have taken you."

"I have an appointment. It took so long to leave that we're going to have to go straight there, rather than the dress shop."

"You have an appointment." Kai drawled. He sounded like he didn't believe her.

"Yes. I have an appointment."

Kai didn't answer. His expression told Connie he wasn't pleased.

"Did you want to go in too?" Connie asked him. Kai quickly shook his head.

"No. I'll wait in the truck."

Connie smothered a smile. She figured he wouldn't go in. Ellen wouldn't have to worry about him telling Maxwell and Breccan what was wrong before she could. Hopefully he wouldn't call them and tell them where Ellen was.

"Okay. It shouldn't be too long. Dr. Schmidt is really good about keeping his appointments on time," Ellen said. "Then we can go look at gowns."

No one spoke, the silence comfortable. Connie could feel the heat coming from Kai's thigh. Each bump along the road sent her leg rubbing against his. Heat streaked from each contact. Connie swallowed. The squeaks from the truck were the only sounds, when Kai spoke up. Thank goodness. She really needed to take her mind off jumping Kai's bones.

"I'll go in both places. I'll sit in the waiting room.

I don't want you two on your own."

Connie and Ellen exchanged glances at Kai's sudden change of mind. Connie hoped Kai would stay unaware of the reason they were there, but with his decision to go in after all, she wasn't sure Ellen would be able to keep him in the dark.

"I understand," Ellen fidgeted.

Connie knew Ellen hoped he would stay with the truck. It would just seem suspicious if they tried to keep him from coming in. After all, Ellen probably just had a summer bug going around. No big deal.

The rest of the drive was accomplished in relative silence. The whirl of the tires on the asphalt road and the wind as it whistled through the open window the only sounds. Kai's heat pulled Connie close. She snuggled into him, burrowing into his side. He smiled down at her and put an arm around her, pulling her in close. She could so get used to this.

****

Kai tightened his arm around her. Her subtle sent

wafted to his nose. Today she smelled like roses. Her curves rested against him, jostling a bit with each bump in the road. He felt more content than in a long time. His dragon wasn't demanding anything, rather he rumbled with contentment. He knew he had his mate with him. It was just a matter of time before she succumbed.

The road into town seemed much too short. The companionable silence was relaxing and having Connie snuggled against him felt right. His hand ran up and down her thigh. Silky soft, he loved the feel of her beneath his hand. Tempting to find out what she wore under that flirty little excuse for a dress, but, with Ellen there, he restrained himself.

He knew Breccan and Maxwell didn't know about the appointment. They were extremely careful of Ellen. He wondered what was up. He would call and let them know where they were when Ellen went in to see the doctor.

Kai entered town, keeping an eye out for pedestrians. He pulled into a parking stall in front of the clinic. "Here we are." He opened his door and exited, slamming it shut and went to help Ellen and Connie down.

He held Ellen's hand as she jumped down. Kai shook his head, she never wanted to wait for help. Connie slid over the seat toward the door. Kai kept an eye on Ellen heading to the sidewalk.

Turning his attention to Connie, once Ellen was safe, Kai grasped her by her waist, pulling her gently from the truck. He smiled as he slid her down his body, trapping her against the seat. Her rose scent deepening, her curves caressing him. He could feel her body soften, feel the hardness of her nipples through her dress as they pressed against his chest. His hands tightened and he lowered his head to taste her.

"Come on, I don't have all day," Ellen hollered at them.

Kai stopped and then shrugged, ignoring Ellen. He needed to taste the honey sweetness of his mate's mouth. Her lips soft, tasting of peppermint from the gloss she applied in the truck. They parted, inviting him in. He needed little invitation, his tongue exploring the textures of her mouth.

"Come on, you two! Let's get going." Kai could

hear the exasperation in Ellen's voice. He reluctantly pulled away from Connie, setting her on the ground.

"Someone's impatient." Placing his hand on her waist, Kai guided Connie around the door, shutting it and clicking the lock on the key fob. "We better get going."

Connie giggled and slapped her hand over her mouth, shaking her head. "You drive me crazy."

Kai grinned and said nothing. Ushering Ellen and Connie inside the clinic, he sat down to wait. Connie and Ellen, heads together, chatted as they went to register Ellen. They seemed too happy to have anything seriously wrong with Ellen. Maybe it was just a routine checkup and she didn't want Breccan hovering. He could at least give her that.

Checking in with the receptionist, Ellen talked low enough Kai couldn't hear. She must have finally figured out how well shifters hear over distance. Connie stood next to her, her hair gleaming and her dress emphasizing her figure. Her legs drew his eyes. The muscles in her legs were sleek, her skin tan and gleaming with health. He wanted to draw them up around his waist and slide into her depths.

Connie turned and smiled at him over her shoulder. Ellen spun around, wobbled and Connie grabbed her arm. Kai watched Ellen shake her off as she headed toward him. Connie shook her head and followed.

"What was that about?"

"I just lost my balance. You know me. I've always been clumsy." Ellen sat down, picked up an outdated magazine and began to look through it.

Kai grunted. Ellen always had been clumsy. Connie attempted to sit on the opposite side of Ellen, away from him. He snagged her arm, pulling her into the seat between them.

"Hey! I can sit where I want. Don't be so bossy." She remained seated, however.

She narrowed her eyes at his smug grin. Kai didn't bother to reply, he'd gotten his way.

She leaned over, grabbed a magazine, giving him the cold shoulder. Feisty mate.

The nurse called Ellen's name and she stood up. Grabbing Connie's hand, she pulled her along to the back of the offices.

"Come on, you're going with me."

Kai kicked back, enjoying the view as Connie and Ellen walked away.

CHAPTER TEN

"Why can't I wait with Kai?"

"I thought you were mad at him? Besides, I want you with me."

"Fine, but I'm not mad at Kai. I'm just trying to exasperate him." She couldn't help the laughter in her voice. "I like to see him riled up."

Ellen laughed. "You better be careful. He's not as easy going as mine."

"I'll be fine. I'm pretty sure I can defuse him." She grinned. Just thinking of ways, sent her belly doing summersaults.

"Were you able to defuse him earlier?"

Connie made a face and stuck out her tongue.

Ellen laughed. "I thought not."

"Let's get your weight, Ellen." The nurse waived her toward the scale. Connie snickered. It was the same type of scale they used in the veterinary clinics. Examining it more closely, it was a bit different, the edges were ramped, perhaps for patients in wheel chairs.

The nurse wrote down the number and ushered Ellen off. "Follow me. I just need to get your blood pressure and heart rate." She escorted them to a nondescript room. The table with stirrups sat like an elephant in the corner. A hazardous waste can abutted the sink. Neatly lined up were the Purell, tissues and cups on the counter. Plain and sterile smelling, the only sign of life in the room were the pictures of the children on the counter.

Typical Scandinavian descendants based on their coloring. The Dutch and German abounded out here. Some of the towns' people still spoke the languages of the old countries. Mainly, the elderly, those that arrived through Ellis Island. They proudly made sure their children learned English, grateful to have landed safely in

America.

Wisconsin included a large population of Native Americans so perhaps that should have been the native language, not English. Connie shook her head, think of Ellen, not tangents. The distraction was welcome, though. Every little bit kept her mind off her reaction to Kai.

The nurse left, telling them the doctor would be in shortly.

"Okay, what gives? Why did you want me here? Not that I mind, but I know you."

Ellen laughed. "Weren't you listening when I talked to the nurse?"

"Well, no. I was checking out the room."

Ellen shook her head. "Sure you were."

"I was. I realized it was as bland as every other doctor's office I've ever visited," Connie said. "Blah, blah, blah."

Ellen laughed and started to speak when a rap tattooed the door. It opened and the doctor stepped in.

"Well, Ellen, I've got a cup for you to pee in. Go do that and head back here. I'll return when the test results are done."

"Thanks, Doc." Ellen grabbed the cup and headed out. The doctor held the door for her. He turned his head toward Connie.

"You can wait here. Ellen should be right back and the results won't take long." Connie nodded as he left, leaving the door cracked for Ellen.

She sat, wondering what she missed and thinking of possibilities. She didn't have long to wait for Ellen to return.

"That was fast."

"I really needed to go." Ellen smiled. "Now, we wait."

"For what?" Connie had an inkling, after adding up the events of the day, but she was more familiar with animal physiology than human.

"Since you missed the conversation with the nurse, you'll have to suffer."

Connie rolled her eyes. "Sure, I'll suffer." They grinned at each other.

"You're such a snot." The amusement in her voice belayed Ellen's words. They settled down, discussing dress ideas for the wedding.

Another rat a tat tat interrupted them. The doctor once again stuck his head in, followed by the rest of his lanky body. His tall frame and red-gold hair marked him as the father of the two in the pictures.

"Well, I have the results." He smiled at Ellen. "Congratulations. Now, let's figure out when the stork will be visiting you."

Connie shrieked, hugging Ellen. Tears formed in her eyes as they did in Ellen's. "Oh my God! A baby! Oh, congratulations, Ellen!"

"I'm so excited!" Ellen's voice was muffled as she hugged Connie back.

"All right, have a seat." The girls gave a last embrace and sat, smiles beaming and tears of happiness on their cheeks. "I definitely see it's good news."

The doctor smiled, going from boy next door cuteness to downright hot with the dimple that appeared in his cheeks. Connie blinked. That was unexpected.

"So, Ellen, any idea when the baby was conceived?"

Connie couldn't help but snort. Ellen and Breccan

went at it like rabbits. Ellen shot her a glare as she answered.

"Not really."

"Well, when was your last menstrual cycle?"

Ellen chewed her lip, thinking. "Maybe, two or three months ago? I'm not really sure."

"Well, how long have you been having morning sickness?"

"At least a couple of months, I think at any rate. I don't get sick every day."

"Hmm, lay down on the bench. Let's see if we can find out." The doctor pulled out a paper blanket. "Put this over your lap and pull up your dress over your belly." The doctor turned and picked up the phone. He spoke into it, asking the nurse to bring some equipment in. "I'm going to do an abdominal ultrasound. It won't hurt you or the baby." He snapped on gloves and turned back. "Have you ever had one?"

"No. I've heard of them and I've seen a few pictures. My parents have one of me."

He chuckled. "The pictures have definitely improved." There was another knock on the door and the nurse entered, pushing a machine and stand that stood taller than her. "Oh, good. Here it is." He turned to Ellen. "We just got a new machine. You get to be our first guinea pig, er patient."

Connie snorted, amused. The doctor looked like a little boy with a new toy.

"Good." Ellen smiled. She radiated happiness. Connie's heart clenched. She wasn't sure she'd ever seen Ellen this happy. Shifters or not, Connie was thankful that Breccan and Maxwell found Ellen and embraced her into their lives.

"This will be cold." The doctor squeezed out an aqua colored gel and dripped it on to Ellen. She flinched and yelped. "Told you." Ignoring her snort, he rubbed it over her abdomen, spreading it thin. "This is to allow the ultrasound to read easier."

The nurse handed the doctor what looked like a microphone. The machine began to beep. He upended it, tracing across Ellen's stomach. Both the girl's eyes shot to the screen. It was fuzzy, more with white noise than anything recognizable.

"Here's your liver, your spleen, those look good."

Ellen and Connie looked at each other and rolled their eyes. "I saw that. I suppose you want to get to the good stuff?"

"Yes." Ellen couldn't say it fast enough.

"Fine." He moved the wand lower and toward her pelvic bone. "Here you go." You could hear the smile in his voice.

Connie was stunned into silence. She grabbed Ellen's hand and held tight. She couldn't believe what she was seeing. It looked just like a real picture. Who knew?

"Um. What exactly am I looking at?" Ellen sounded as stunned as Connie. "Are you sure that's not malfunctioning?" Connie could hear her gulp.

"Not a chance." The doctor laughed. "I'd say you're having a litter."

Ellen shot him a dirty look. "That's not funny." She turned her head to Connie. "Oh, my God. How will I handle three of them? I'm going to kill Breccan!"

Connie laughed. "You'll have plenty of help. You know it. One baby for each of you and one for Maxwell."

At that, Ellen smiled, if a little evilly.

"You're right. They'll each have to be responsible for a baby, for everything. Dirty diapers and all." Ellen laughed. "Can I get a picture, Doc?"

He shook his head, smiling. "You sure can. I'd say your litter." He laughed at Ellen's glare, "Er, bundles of joy should be coming somewhere around February. You look about two, maybe three months along." He fiddled with the machine. "How many pictures do you want?"

"Five?" She looked at Connie who nodded. "Five."

"Not a problem." The machine started spitting out pictures. "Let's get you cleaned up." The nurse came over and wiped Ellen down, removing the gel, then handed her a sterile wipe to clean off anything she missed.

"Congratulations, Ellen."

Ellen smiled. The news was good, even if it was an overabundance of good. Connie was thrilled for her cousin.

"Let's get you down." The doctor held his hands out to Ellen, keeping her steady as she sat up and maneuvered down from the bench. "I'll leave you to get straightened up and be back in a minute." The doctor left, closing the door behind him.

"Oh, my God, Ellen! Can you believe it?"

"No. Three babies." Ellen looked stunned. "Connie, how am I going to handle three babies? Really?"

Connie gave her a quick hug. "One at a time, Ellen. You'll have plenty of help."

"Breccan's never touching me again."

Connie laughed. "I'm sure. Come on, let's get you seated." The girls sat, the silence in the office filled with wonder. Connie glanced down and rubbed a hand over her stomach. How would Kai react if it was her? Her breath caught. She just knew he'd be thrilled.

"You so have to get the transfer to UW." Ellen slid a glance at her. "How on earth will I cope?"

"Like your mom is going to leave you alone." Connie elbowed her. "Her first grandchildren. You'll be her golden girl."

Ellen giggled. "Three grandchildren. Mom will be in heaven."

The tap on the door came, heralding the doctor. "Well, Ellen, I've a few things to discuss with you." He swung down into his chair. "You need to get started on prenatal vitamins. I've a sample here and I've called in the prescription to your pharmacy." Doctor Schmidt handed a bottle to Ellen. He then pulled the ultrasound photos toward him. "It's too early to tell the sex of the babies. That is, if you wanted to know."

"When will we be able to check?"

"Usually twenty weeks or more. But multiples are harder to determine. It gets pretty crowded in there. I plan on monitoring you carefully. Multiple births present risks to the mother and fetuses. One of the risks is that labor will be early, too early, endangering the fetuses. Only one in ten thousand births are triplets or greater. The gestation period for triplets is around thirty two weeks and the babies may very well require incubation."

"But they'll be okay?"

"Multiple births carry risks, Ellen. Our best bet is to ensure you are healthy enough to carry the babies as close to term as possible."

"Doc, is there a difference if the father is a shifter?" Connie asked. Ellen looked grateful at the question. She felt guilty. She wanted to know for Ellen's sake, but for hers too. It never hurt to have information.

"I don't know. Perhaps. I've never really investigated. Ellen is the first one I know to have a multiple shifter pregnancy." He sat back. "But that could be because I'm not a shifter doctor. I could find one and recommend one to you." He stared at the wall. "I think I will do that. I'll still monitor you, but I think it would be a good thing to have you see a shifter doctor also." He grinned, coming back to the present. "Better safe than sorry. Do you have any questions?"

"How often will I have to come and see you? Will vitamins be enough? Do I need to add anything to my diet?"

"Can she still have sex?" Connie grinned. She figured she might as well ask. Breccan rarely left Ellen untouched.

"Connie!"

Doctor Schmidt laughed. "I think once a month for the next few months since you're carrying multiples. If you have any concerns call immediately to make an appointment. You should make sure you eat lots of vegetables and proteins. Spinach, anything high in folic acid to aid in growth and development. And yes, you can still have sex." He opened the drawer of the desk. "Here are some pamphlets that will let you know what foods you should be eating, what you need to look out for, warning signs if you will. Call if you have questions."

He stood up.

"Thank you, Doctor Schmidt." Ellen took the pamphlets he offered. "How fast do you think I'll grow in a month?"

"With three? In another month you should look like you've swallowed a basketball." Ellen groaned. "Oh, no. How will we be able to order dresses?"

"Dresses?" The doctor looked confused.

Connie spoke up. "Don't worry, Ellen, we'll figure it out." She looked at the doc. "Ellen's getting married in a month."

"Best of luck. At least the father will be around to support you."

Ellen nodded, looking a bit stunned.

"Don't forget to set up your next appointment. I'll call when I have a shifter doctor for you." He smiled and left, leaving the door open.

"Connie, what am I going to do?"

"You're going to get married and have babies, Ellen. What you've always wanted to do." Connie bounced from foot to foot. Babies. In. The. House. Connie couldn't wait to go shopping.

Ellen turned and hugged her. "You're right, Connie. I just have to believe everything will be okay." Shoving the vitamins and papers in her purse, she stood, grabbed the photos, smiled and tucked them away also.

They headed out of the office and stopped at the appointment desk on the way back to Kai.

****

Kai lifted his head. Close to an hour passed. Finally Connie and Ellen headed down the hall, closer to the waiting room. He could smell their scents coming toward him. He frowned, watching them come into view. They appeared to be bursting with excitement and a bit of trepidation. He watched them stop at the receptionist. Ellen appeared to be making another appointment.

He'd have to tell Breccan, unless Ellen did it first. He'd give her the chance. The girls both seemed excited, so it couldn't be bad news. They seemed giddy, smiles wreathing their faces. Kai stood, silently escorting them to the truck. It was obvious they shared a secret. It remained to be seen what the secret was.

"Do you still want to head to the wedding boutique?" Kai asked while Ellen and Connie looked at each other, smiling.

"No. I think we'll do that another day." Ellen seemed to glow. "I think I want to go home and see my man." Connie gave a soft laugh and grabbed Ellen's hand.

"I think that's a good idea." Her voice dropped into a whisper. "He'll be so excited."

He helped them in, then got behind the wheel. Kai draped an arm around Connie, pulling her tight into his side. He enjoyed the warmth she generated as she snuggled up to him. They drove in silence, Kai more content than in a long time. Ellen played with the radio until she found a station she liked and began singing along to a song she recognized. Kai winced, the sound of her voice, just slightly off key.

"Knock it off! You're hurting Kai's ears." Connie glanced at Ellen, jabbing her with her elbow. "I don't think country is your type of music."

"But I like it." Ellen grinned. "Are you saying I can't carry a tune?" Ellen started warbling and the noise got worse.

"I thought you could sing." Kai swore he'd heard better from her. Maybe it was just the country music. If everyone could sing it, there would be more stations.

Ellen laughed and began again, this time in perfect tune.

Kai swung a look at her, a bit disgusted. She could sing, so she must have been doing it just to aggravate them.

"Sorry, got tired of being the third wheel with you two snuggling up." Ellen grinned at him. "I figured that would catch your attention." Kai snorted and shook his head. Pulling Connie closer, he continued the drive in silence, listening to the women chatter. He noticed they never mentioned why Ellen went to the doctor.

Pulling in the drive, Kai saw Breccan and Maxwell

sitting at the house. Standing as he pulled to a stop, Breccan headed to open Ellen's door.

"I'm going to talk to them." Ellen slid down, into Breccan's arms. "I'll see you later."

"Right! How about I take care of supper and you can take your time?" Connie leaned out the door to holler at Ellen as she headed into the house.

"You're on!"

Grinning, Connie sat back.

Kai slid out of the truck and pulled her toward him. Sliding her out, he pulled her tight against him. He closed his eyes, savoring the soft warmth of her body, and the scent that clung to her skin. Her arms wrapped around his neck and she buried her nose in his neck. Her breath tickling his skin.

"So, you want to tell me what's going on?" He felt Connie giggle against his neck.

"I guess it'd be okay. Ellen's obviously telling Breccan." Connie rubbed her nose along the crease of his neck. She let out a soft puff of air, which raised the hair on his nape. Kai rubbed his cheek against the top of her head. Much as he wanted her, just holding Connie made him happy.

"So?"

"Ellen's pregnant." Connie laughed softly. "With a litter. That's what the doctor said."

Kai pulled back and looked at her, his brow raised.

"Triplets." She snickered, burying her face against his neck again.

Kai smiled. "Well, she did mate a dog. Wolves often have multiples. So do dragons. I have a brother and sister." Connie pulled back looking at him, quirking a brow in question. "You'll be working with one of them. But I haven't heard from my sister in years. She drops in once a decade or so."

"Triplets."

"Yes." Kai laughed at the expression on her face. "Don't ever forget, Connie, we are animals." Kai held tight as she tried to push out of his arms. He laughed at the expression on her face, a moue of distaste.

"That's not funny." Her voice was low.

"It wasn't meant to be. But we are what we are. Sometimes the animal can take over." He nuzzled her neck. "Especially when you taste and smell so good." He rumbled, the growl causing her to shiver in his arms. He pulled her close and she melted against his body, tucking her head under his chin.

"I just can't seem to resist you," Connie murmured.

Kai felt a thrill run through him, a sense of triumph. Maybe it wouldn't take much more until she was willing to admit she was his mate. He wasn't willing to give her up, but he was willing to give her the time to accept him. There was no other option for him. He waited centuries for her. A month or two would seem like no time at all.

"I'm glad you realize we were meant to be together." His satisfaction oozed through his words. It didn't mean he wouldn't try to get a rise out of her.

Connie pulled her head back. Even with his eyes closed he could feel her glare.

"Don't worry, I'll give you all the time you need." It was so easy to tease her. Kai looked at her and smirked. When sparks flew from her eyes, he thought about what a magnificent dragon she would be.

"Just because I can't resist you doesn't mean that

at all." Her nose met his, her eyes crossing with the effort of glaring into his.

"Just give me time to prove it. That's all I ask." Kai leaned forward, following her head as she leaned back. Sliding a hand up, cupping the soft curve of her head, he stilled her movement. "Just give me a chance." Leaning deeper, looking into her clear blue gaze, Kai kissed her. Sank into the softness of her lips, the moist silkiness that drove him crazy and kissed her like there was no tomorrow. There would be though, he would make sure of it.

CHAPTER ELEVEN

Connie got ready for work. Her stomach twisting and turning in anticipation. The lost internship at Brookfield was hard to swallow, but at least she would still be learning. Thinking of why she lost it, Connie regretted the loss, but perked up. She was glad to be alive. Certain the guys were going a little overboard on security, she couldn't help but be happy about it. They made her feel safer. Troubled by bouts of paranoia, she kept looking over her shoulder with an eerie sense of being watched. She shivered, her stomach knotting.

Kai stared, but it wasn't the same. His stare made her preen. Connie giggled, her mood lightening. Kai seemed to love her sundresses, and she loved teasing him. Breccan and Maxwell became even more protective once Ellen told them she was pregnant. Idly, she wondered what their story was. Shaking her head, Connie made her bed, running her hand along the pillows.

Connie was glad she only worried about Kai. She'd awoken both mornings with only an indent in the pillow next to her in bed proving she hadn't slept alone. She pouted. He seemed to be able to resist her charms just fine. Kai seemed to come in after she was asleep and leave before she woke.

She shook her head, snorting. Kai was too darn irresistible. Who knew what he could talk her into? Lucky for her he wasn't coming into her room while she was awake. Connie knew she wouldn't be able to say no to anything he asked. She tossed her head. No need to let him know that, though.

Connie finished pulling her hair back into a bun. Left down, it would end up chewed or slimed from the animals. Her first time working at a vet's, she'd learned her lesson. Her hair went up and hopefully it stayed that way. She grabbed her Croc's. Ugly, but comfortable, when on her feet all day. Snatching her purse, Connie headed out of her room to grab a quick breakfast before she left. She'd keep it light, anticipation making her a bit queasy.

Hanging her purse on the chair, she opened the fridge. Grabbing a yogurt and a banana, she poured a cup of coffee in a travel mug sitting empty on the counter. She sniffed, Ellen added a yummy peppermint to the mug. The hot liquid sent the scent circulating. With a deep breath, the smell alone waking her, Connie sat. She ate, taking appreciative sips of her coffee, making sure to get a bit of caffeine into her system.

"Are you almost ready?" Kai stepped in the door.

Connie looked up. "Just let me finish. I assume you still insist on driving?" She cocked a brow at him. He looked yummy this morning. His plaid shirt unbuttoned, showing off his ripped abs. A ripple of desire shook her. He grinned. Damn those dragon senses!

"Yes. I want to make sure you're safe." The bit of

growl in his voice, made her heart beat faster. Looking at his groin, she knew she wasn't the only one effected.

"I'll be fine." She sounded breathless. She cleared her throat. Maybe that would help.

"Plus, I want to see my brother." He ignored her.

Connie rolled her eyes and snorted. She wasn't mute, darn it. How did she find him so attractive?

"What?" Kai raised his brow at her. Damn, he was sexy, even when he was being bossy.

"You've had plenty of time to see him. Why now?" Connie knew why. Kai was pig-headed. She'd be safe at work. He just wanted to press his claim in front of the men there. The pig.

"You're not going by yourself. I told you that."

"You're not the boss of me." Connie stuck her tongue out. "You can't tell me what to do."

"Wrong. I can and I will. Until I'm sure you are safe."

She stood and tossed her peel and yogurt cup in the trash. Grabbing the mug, Connie refreshed it. "I'm ready."

Kai held open the door for her. "Then let's go."

The ride was uneventful. Kai sat behind the wheel, grabbed her and pulled her into his side. Connie mentally squirmed. She wanted to melt into his side, but didn't want to encourage him. Thoughts of Kai over shadowed the nervousness of starting a new job. She almost felt obsessed. She was beginning to crave him, his hands on her, his mouth nibbling every part of her. She'd never reacted to another man like that. But he was so damn bossy. And old. She couldn't forget old.

The road was ending, town coming closer. The last few days of being around Kai were surreal. It didn't seem possible for a man to get under her skin like this. Shaking her head, she continued looking out the window.

"What was that thought?"

"What?"

"The one that made you shake your head."

"Nothing." She twisted her lips in a moue. "Well, it all just seems crazy. You, the bad guys, Ellen and her wolves. This is not my life." She looked up at Kai. "I don't know how to handle it."

Kai eased the truck into the parking lot. "Just let me keep you safe. The rest will work out. Remember, you're my mate, and I'm willing to give you time. I know it will work out in the end."

Connie wanted to shake him in exasperation. "I don't know I'm your mate. You can say it all you want. It doesn't make it so." His slow grin, the quirk of his lips, made her want to taste them. Knowing that's the last thing she should do, she shook her head. "You just don't give up, do you?"

"Remember that." Kai opened his door and slid out. He pulled Connie toward him and helped her out, keeping his hands on her waist. She wouldn't let him see how the touch of his hands shot warmth above and below. His touch made her feel cherished and protected. Peeking up, she figured he might already know, if the satisfied look on his face was anything to judge by. He was exasperating, but oh, so, mouthwatering.

Kai lowered his head and took her mouth in a slow, sensuous kiss. The feel of his firm lips against hers made her groan. The teasing edge of his teeth nibbled on her lips before his tongue swooped in, exploring the sensitive interior of her mouth. Connie could feel her nipples tighten, the thin top of her scrubs and lacy bra too little a barrier for the heat emanating from his chest. He lifted his head, breaking the kiss and pulled her up, wrapping her legs around him before sliding his hands to her bottom.

"You wore panties." The hoarse tone of his voice made her giggle.

She tightened her arms around his neck.

"As much as I want to take this further." Kai slipped a finger inside her waistband, and stroked her skin. "You have to get to work." With another teasing slide of his finger, Kai kissed her deeply and set her down. "We'll continue this later." He patted her on the ass and walked toward the door, stopping to glance back at her.

Connie watched him walk, swagger in every step he took. She shook her head, and with a smile, headed to the door, ignoring the arousal he generated. Kai was damn cocky, but boy did he have reason. Just a kiss ignited her, sending her body up in flames. He held the door, ushering her inside. He shut it, following her in, the ringing bell announcing their presence.

The appointment desk sat empty. Connie could

hear the rumble of voices in the back room. She looked around, not sure where to go. She knew better than to barge into an examination room without knowing what animal was in there. Especially as the clinic specialized in exotics. She looked around. Kai stood lounging against the desk. She paced nervously and turned to sit in one of the chairs that comprised the waiting area. Multi-colored hard plastic chairs lined one side of the room. Easy cleanup. As a veterinary assistant, she'd cleaned up her share of vomit and piss from sick pets. Occasionally blood, but it was rare a fight would break out. This waiting room looked well thought out, clean and healthy.

"So, they knew you were coming, right?" Kai's words brought her attention back to him.

"Of course." Connie rolled her eyes at the skeptical note in his voice.

"Then where are they?" Kai glanced around, his chest puffing up, a frown on his face.

"They'll be out when they're ready. You can't just leave an animal on its own. I don't know what they are dealing with. You can go home, you know." Connie waved toward the door.

"I'll wait until they come out. I'm not leaving you on your own. Besides, no reason I can't say hello to my brother." Kai smiled, and no matter how innocent he tried to look, she knew he was up to something.

"Connie, you're here." The veterinarian walked out from in back. He entered the waiting room and turned his head sharply, looking straight at Kai. "Well, well, look what the cat dragged in." He turned and headed to Kai, stopping just in front of him and sniffed. A grin broke out on his face. "I thought that's who I smelled on her. Is she your mate then?"

"Yes."

"No."

His head swiveled between them as his smile widened. "So, Kai, which is it?"

"Yes, she just doesn't want to admit it."

Connie rolled her eyes. The stubborn man. She was not giving him the satisfaction of agreeing. She had her future to think of, but she didn't want to lose him either. There was plenty of time to figure it out. She was young and Kai was, well she didn't really know, except that he was at least as old as her grandfather and that was just ick when she thought about it. So, no agreement with the hot, old fart. Connie grinned and wondered what he'd do if she called him that.

"Welcome, Connie. Kai, did you need anything else? A distemper shot maybe?"

"Always thought you were a comedian, didn't you? Lucky you didn't decide to do that for a living." Kai laughed and gave him a hug. "Aidan, make sure you take care of my mate. Don't let her leave until I come back for her. She could be in danger."

"I'm sure we'd know if they found me." Connie shook her head. "How would they even know I'd be here? I'll be fine. Go home."

"What danger?" Aidan shot Kai a frown and turned to her.

"I witnessed a murder and due to a screw up at the police station, I was followed home. I got away and came up to visit my cousin. My brother just wanted to warn me to be careful. I doubt they'd follow me up here, even if they knew where here was."

"Her brother is a police man and he's worried. Keep an eye on her." Kai just had to add his two cents.

Hopefully, Aidan wouldn't fire her on the spot.

Connie wanted to groan in frustration. Dr. Aidan leaned toward Kai and they spoke in low whispers, too low for her to hear what they were saying. No doubt it was about her safety. The men shook hands and pulled each other into a hug. Looking at them side by side, Connie admitted they were a couple of handsome men, though Kai was just a bit yummier to her.

"I'll see you tonight when I pick Connie up."

"Sounds good. Nice to see you're holding up so well for your age." Aidan's grin flashed.

"You should talk." The laughter threaded Kai's voice. "You're the same age."

"You're still the big brother and don't you forget it." He slapped Kai's back. "Now, I have an assistant to train and work to get to. So, go away."

Kai laughed. He stopped, grabbed Connie and gave her a quick kiss. "Don't leave without me." The bell ringing as he exited.

Connie turned to the vet. "Good morning." She smiled, her nervousness coming back in full force. "Sorry about that." She waved her hands, motioning toward the door where Kai left.

"No worries. Kai tends to plow over people." The amusement unmistakable in his voice.

Connie nodded her head fervently in agreement. "I know." She exhaled, relieved Doc wasn't going to fire her before she began.

Aidan laughed. "Come on, you can put your things back here. Lou cleaned out a locker for you in the break room." He turned and headed into the back, Connie trailing behind, looking everywhere she could.

She tried to stop bouncing, barely able to contain herself. She couldn't wait to begin. She just knew she'd learn a lot here.

Aidan saw her gazing around. "I'll take you on a tour shortly. I made sure to make time to get you settled before the first patient."

Connie smiled, wiping her palms discretely on her pants. She had a feeling she was going to enjoy it here.

****

From the window of the coffee shop next door,

Fred watched the woman enter the vet clinic. She and the man with her didn't have a pet. When the man left without her, he didn't waste time. Tossing his empty cup in the trash he stepped outside and pulled out his phone. When it was answered he spoke.

"I think I found our target." He listened. "No, I'm pretty sure it's her. She just went into a veterinary clinic, but she didn't have an animal with her." He nodded. "Oh, that makes sense. So she probably just went to work." He listened, nodding his head. "Yeah, I can do that. Okay, I'll call you later." He hung up, sliding his phone back in his pocket. Heading to his car and reaching inside, Fred pulled out a laptop. Looking at the clinic, he turned and headed back inside and ordered another cup of coffee. He leaned against the counter while he waited.

"Do you have Wi-Fi?" He gestured to his laptop. "I thought I'd work while I enjoyed my coffee and just relax a while."

The clerk nodded. "We do. It's not a problem at all." She tapped a sign on the wall. "This is the Wi-Fi and password." She handed him his coffee and smiled. "Enjoy and take all the time you need. There's no rush."

"Thanks, Meg." Her name tag told her name. He might as well try to stay on her good side. Maybe she'd give him more information on his target. She appeared to know them from what he'd seen the last time he'd been here.

"Your welcome." Her face lit up in reply.

Fred set up his computer, keeping an eye out the window. He saw the truck that the woman arrived in, circle back in the lot and leave again. He sat back, watching. When the truck didn't return, he resumed sipping his coffee and keeping an eye on the clinic. Quiet as the coffee shop was, he could easily spend the day here. Fred sat back and surfed the net, keeping busy, while keeping an eye on the clinic, waiting for the target to reappear. Now that he located where she was, it would be a simple matter to follow her home, just to make sure he was staking out the right property.

Wanting a cup of coffee before he did reconnaissance, he went to the only shop in town. Seeing the woman he hunted come in while he relaxed there was serendipitous. Fred hadn't seen her since though. The barista was closed mouthed when he'd asked about her.

Perhaps it didn't sound as idle as he hoped. If he got on her good side maybe she'd offer more information.

He opened his email and perused the information on the target. If he couldn't follow her home, he would check the addresses of her family. He could easily drive around and find out where they lived. If she stayed at one of their houses, it would be a simple matter to get her. He thought she was out of town, staying on that dirty little farm, but if he was wrong, it would make his job a whole lot simpler. He needed to be sure.

The coffee shop saw a steady clientele. No one stayed too long and no one bothered him. Fred kept to himself, appearing engrossed in his computer, refilling his coffee and even ordering lunch. The day passed, no one giving him more than a passing glance. His nostrils flared, the aroma of fresh brewed coffee and the sticky sweetness of the specialty coffees permeating the air. With a deep breath, he sat back and glanced at his watch. He didn't see her leave even for lunch. It was just after 2:00 PM. He wasn't sure how long he could continue to sit here.

The barista kept glancing over at him for the last

half hour or so. He didn't want to strike up a conversation and she appeared ready to do just that. Glancing from her to the window, he saw the truck that dropped her off, pull in. The man that dropped his target off this morning arrived and jumped out, walking to the door and into the veterinary clinic.

Closing his computer, Fred put it away, stood and threw out his trash. Sliding it in his satchel, Fred waved at the barista, trying to keep his face friendly and exited the shop. He hid his excitement. Opening his car, he put his computer on the passenger seat and got in, trying to appear innocuous.

He looked, but couldn't see the license plate of the truck from this angle. He pulled slowly out and when he could see the plate without being obvious he parked again and lifted his phone to his ear. He quickly wrote down the plate and dialed. A familiar voice answered. One that would do what he needed.

"I need you to run a plate for me." He kept his voice low, cautious even with no one around.

"Why?" The voice was low, obviously he was trying not to be heard. "You're not supposed to call me here."

"Don't ask questions. You're getting paid and no one will even know."

"Give me the number."

Fred rattled it off. "It's a Wisconsin plate."

"That might take a bit more time. If I can get it without tipping any one off I will."

"Find a way. I'll be waiting." Fred hung up the phone and sat. It shouldn't be too much longer before the pair came out of the clinic. His target got away from him in Chicago, but he didn't plan on losing her this time. Careful planning would get him what he wanted. Following her to the apartment in Chicago a spur of the moment action, something an amateur would do and it showed. Fred knew better, but took the chance when it presented itself. He prided himself on always being ready. That didn't mean it always worked out.

He sat, watching the clinic, his car engine a low rumble in his ears. A short time later, the pair came out. Rather than opening the passenger door, the man escorted her to the driver's side, lifting her up and climbing in after her. After what looked like a steamy embrace, the man put on his seatbelt and started the engine. With a turn of his head, probably looking for nonexistent traffic, he backed up and pulled out.

Fred waited until they were partially down the block before he pulled out. He followed, trying to keep a low profile. The last thing he wanted to do was be seen. When the truck turned to head out of town, Fred passed the intersection, not turning. He saw the man glancing in the rear view mirror and to the sides. If the man was spooked, Fred didn't want to tip his hand. The license plate would give him a name and address. He had time.

****

Kai slowly backed out of the parking lot, eyes on the alert. He despised the idea of leaving Connie in town, but knew his brother Aidan would watch out for her. Not to mention the fact the other employee was also a shifter, a hyena if he wasn't mistaken, and Kai knew she should be safe. Should be. There was very little that would intimidate either of them. But still, she was his mate, no matter her arguments. Kai knew the best one to protect her was him. His dragon agreed. Connie however, didn't. He grudgingly agreed to stay away. He'd just have to kick his brother's ass if anything went wrong.

Kai's gut ached upon leaving her. It could be the fact Connie was not under his eye, but Kai decided to make sure before he left her for the day. He pulled out and circled the block. Coming back to the drive, he decided to check out the parking lot. It led around to the side of the clinic, ending at a loading dock. Looking at it, Kai realized the door was built to allow a dragon to enter or exit. That may not have been the original intentions, but it would serve the purpose. He knew his brother earned a medical degree besides the veterinary license. He needed to have both to effectively treat shifters. Aidan combined his degrees before shifters came out.

Seeing nothing to explain his uneasiness, Kai circled the lot. There were a few cars scattered throughout, employees of the different stores and their customers. Nothing to set off any alarms. He would definitely make sure he picked Connie up on time. He didn't want her to wait outside, or decide to wander off without him. He knew her aunt, uncle and grandfather lived nearby. Connie wouldn't even think about it being unsafe to go there and he just wanted her safe until the men after her were caught. Leaving town and Connie behind, Kai turned on the radio and headed home.

His shoulder blades itched pulling away. He wasn't comfortable leaving Connie, but she refused to let him stay. She made that clear on the drive over. The covert amusement from his brother didn't help. He was probably imagining things and he didn't have the time to babysit Connie all day anyway. Not when any threats to her appeared nonexistent. Just a feeling something wasn't right. He growled and reluctantly headed back to the farm.

He took care of business and directed the workers in their assigned tasks. Not that they needed much supervision, most of the hands here since Casey's time. The few migrants, stayed to themselves and worked hard. They lived in the cattle barns most of the time. The migrant workers were barn swallow shifters, spending the winter in the south and heading north to work in the spring and summer. Most of them came year after year, heading up from Texas when it was too hot down there to grow anything. Generations came in, seamlessly replacing the elderly, those too feeble to continue the hard work.

Casey built homes for them away from the main complex. The mated pairs lived there, but the younger ones preferred their bird form when not working. Kai didn't really mind, they tended to keep the insect population down.

Kai headed into the barn office and checked the monitors. There was nothing suspicious in the area. Keeping one eye on the monitors, Kai settled down to enter payroll on the computer. He'd have time to update it before he picked up Connie from work. Since meeting Connie, Kai neglected this part of his job. With Connie at work he made time to enter data and get everything up to date. Ignoring the pull to go to her, he sat down to get to work.

Finished, Kai shut off the computer, his alarm letting him know the time arrived to get ready to pick Connie up from work. Plenty of time to spare since he'd set it earlier than needed. He was just impatient. He glanced at the time. Connie didn't get off of work for another forty-five minutes. No longer willing to wait, Kai figured he might as well be early. He grabbed the truck keys. Outside, he could see Maxwell lounging on the porch, drowsing in the sun. There was no sign of Breccan or Ellen. Kai figured they must be inside, Maxwell on guard now that they knew Ellen was carrying pups.

"I'm heading into town to pick up Connie." He headed toward the wolf. The tension in his body belied his relaxed appearance. Kai knew he would hear him.

"That's good. I know Ellen wants to make sure she's safe."

"By the way, congratulations." Kai grinned at Maxwell.

"Thank you. We're thrilled."

"As you should be." Wolves were pack animals. Any pups guarded from conception to adulthood. No matter whose pups, they belonged to the pack, protected by all.

"Yes." Breccan appeared in the doorway. A deep satisfaction ran through his voice. "Our pack is growing."

Kai grunted. He long considered this area his territory. If Ellen hadn't been Breccan's mate, he would have tried to get them to leave. As it was, the farm produced enough to meet all of their needs, and with their mate owning the property, Kai now considered it theirs, grudgingly. It wasn't easy. Dragons tended to covet anything they touched. His dragon still patrolled the wider area of the county. Though not legally, he couldn't stop believing it all belonged under his protection. Was his. Forever.

"You know that you two will eventually have to take over for me?" Connie would eventually give in to the mating pull and Kai wouldn't think of raising a family on what essentially became the wolves pack land. His land was more than adequate and it wasn't far. It was far superior. It hid natural treasures no one else knew about. Not to mention his hoard remained there.

He knew Connie and Ellen wanted to remain close. He would have to consult an architect to enlarge the original homestead, modernize it. Enlarge it to make room for the family he desired. Once Kai changed her, Connie would like his cavern, but even when she became a dragon, she wouldn't think like one.

"Yes. We know. Especially since Connie is your

mate. Where will you live? I know Ellen would like to have her close."

"I own land near here. Not far."

Breccan nodded. He didn't bother to ask where. Not that he would have told him.

"Time to get Connie. I'll be back later." Kai left, feeling the wolf watch him. He pulled up in front of the clinic, feeling the uneasiness return. Glancing around, he didn't notice anything unusual. He would stay on guard, regardless. Nothing would be allowed to harm his mate. Hopping out, he headed into the clinic.

CHAPTER TWELVE

Connie vibrated with excitement. Thrilled with her day. The doc showed her around the clinic and let her sit in on the appointments he scheduled for the day. She enjoyed seeing the different cases. Most of them were routine, your typical pet inoculations. One snake case came in, it seemed to be off its feed. Aidan decided to keep it overnight for observation. The day went on, and Aidan stood back and let her treat the animals that came in.

"You're doing well. You really have an empathy with animals." His deep voice didn't thrill her like Kai's.

"Thank you, I really enjoyed today." Heat rose in her cheeks. She loved working with animals.

"You're welcome. I think you'll be an asset here. Lou will show you the billing system tomorrow." He looked out the window. "That empathy should really help with my brother." Aidan snickered. "Speak of the devil. So tell me, when are you going to put him out of his misery?"

Connie frowned. "What do you mean?"

"It's obvious you're mates, but haven't done anything about it."

"We are not. He might think so, but I don't do mates. I'm human."

Aidan laughed. "Sure you are. That's okay, my brother needs to work for it, so just keep on telling him that." His eyes gleamed wickedly. "You'll give in eventually. There is no fighting the mating pull."

Connie glared and stamped her foot. "I will decide in my own time. Just because you dragons say I'm his mate means nothing to me." She found it hard to stay mad. The day being just too good, but she wasn't about to let these dragons brow beat her.

"Just because you don't admit it, doesn't mean we're not." Kai's voice startled her. She hadn't heard the bell announcing anyone entering. The warmth of his body behind her melted her bones as his lips descended on her neck, sending shivers down her now non-existent spine. The warmth of his lips and the sharp nip of his teeth made her body heat up, starting an ache between her legs.

"This is not the place to discuss this." She didn't mean to sound so breathy. His chuckle sent a warm breath of air over her neck. Kai stepped to her side, his hands holding hers.

"Aidan, were there any issues today?"

"No. It was a quiet day. Why?"

"Just an uneasy feeling." Kai glanced at Connie. "Don't leave the building by yourself."

Connie gritted her teeth, trying to tug her hand from his. "I'm not a child. I'm aware of the situation." Kai slipped an arm around her waist, pulling her to his side. He was always so warm, all she wanted to do was sink into him. But his attitude. Needed. Work.

His strength made her feel safe, like no one could get to her. Connie never worried about being safe before. Not like now, with someone after her, or supposedly after her. But she didn't want to be wrapped in cotton wool. No matter how nice it sometimes felt. She wouldn't admit it, but she'd felt apprehensive today also. Figuring it was first day on the job nerves. Maybe because she'd known Kai wasn't near. She mentally shook herself. She couldn't let him weasel into her feelings.

Right now, after a good day she felt fine, ecstatic really. Working with animals calmed her. Working with shifters seemed to do the same thing. Maybe because they were part animal. She'd have to keep that in mind when dealing with Kai.

Aidan laughed. "It was probably because you were separated. Especially since you haven't completed your mating bond."

Connie rolled her eyes. She'd heard enough about the mating bond. She wasn't even sure she'd be accepted to go to school here. If necessary she'd finish her year out in Chicago. She wasn't about to lose what she worked so hard for. If she gave in and returned to Chicago, she would have a hard time leaving Kai. Much better to deny all claims and feelings until she knew where she would be going. She could only pray it worked. The ache in her heart at the thought told her it wouldn't be quite so easy.

"I'm working on it." Kai sounded so sure of himself. Connie elbowed him in his side. Her elbow ached from the contact. It was like trying to move a brick wall. He laughed, knowing she meant him to feel the jab. Instead, she felt the repercussions.

"You won't succeed." She sniffed. Connie didn't know why she challenged him. She knew better. Kai patted her on the ass.

"You just keep dreaming, sweetheart." He looked at Aidan. "We'll be back tomorrow." They turned to leave. Aidan grasped Kai's arm.

"Wait." Kai cocked an eyebrow at him in question. "Do you have a lair?"

"Why?"

"I have some questions for you." He looked from Connie's quizzical face back to Kai. "We'll get together later and discuss it." He waved them toward the door. "Have a good night. Connie, we'll see you tomorrow."

"Good night."

"Night, Aidan. I'll call you later." Kai nodded and escorted Connie out the door.

Connie looked between the brothers. She knew she'd missed something. She'd seen Maxwell and Breccan do the same weird thing. Like they were having a private conversation no one else was a part of. Connie exited the clinic beside Kai, studying him.

He was tall and muscular, confident. He affected her like no other man before. He searched the surrounding area as he walked. Not obviously. If she hadn't been looking she might not have noticed. Subconsciously, she trusted him or she doubted he'd make her feel so safe. Everything about him appealed to her. She would seriously need to guard her heart.

Kai opened the driver's side door and pulled her in front of him.

"Time to hop in." Kai grasped her waist and lifted her to the seat.

"You know I can get in by myself." She lifted her

brow at him. She was trying to act cool.

"I know, but then I couldn't do this." Kai pulled her toward the edge of the seat, and placing one hand on the nape of her neck pulled her closer. Connie couldn't help it. She sank into his kiss, seduced by the low tone of his voice, and commanding feel of his hand directing her to his mouth, not to mention the firm touch of his lips gliding over hers.

Wiggling as close as she could, her arms encircled his neck, surrendering without a thought. Her legs wrapped around his body, close enough to feel the imprint of his hard muscles everywhere. She ached for his touch. Kai drew back slowly, swiping his tongue against her lips, drawing an involuntary moan at the burst of heat he left behind. He sat upright nibbling on her jaw.

"Time to head home." He disentangled Connie from him. "Slide over so I can get in."

Connie felt the shiver of lust as her body interpreted the words the way she wanted to hear. She would happily let him slide into her body. His touch caused flames to rage inside her. The feel of his body against hers lit a fuse Connie couldn't extinguish. No matter what she did, her passion would simmer until his next inflammatory touch.

Kai's hand on her ass, shifting her brought her attention back. She slid over, pulling her feet around to sit forward, moving until Kai could slide inside. He sat, pulled on his seatbelt and put the keys in the ignition. Connie snapped on her belt, and snuggled into the warmth of Kai's side as he started the truck and pulled out, heading home.

****

Kai gave himself a quick adjustment, so the drive home wouldn't be so uncomfortable. The tightness of the denim encasing him just made him want to be inside Connie, trading the rough fabric for the hot and creamy depths of her body. He pulled her close, enjoying the weight of her against his side. He didn't think he could wait much longer to be inside her again. He needed her. His desire and the mating call circled inside him, demanding that he stamp his mate as his. Mark her and permeate her pores with his essence so no one could mistake the fact she was taken, she was his.

Just the thought of Connie saturated with his scent, warning off all others made him throb. He felt her hands on him, unconsciously caressing him. The scenery passed with no other traffic on the road. He slowed. No reason not to enjoy the time they were alone.

Connie's hands slid over his crotch, teasing him.

"Connie."

He could hear her stifle a giggle. Her hand slid, caressing him through the denim. He heard a click and she turned to him, sliding so she could use both hands. She pulled down his zipper, freeing his cock from the denim prison. Her soft hand grasped him, cool against the heat emanating from him. He pushed his hips forward, seeking more of her touch.

He jolted when her tongue licked up his length, to tease his cap.

"Connie."

She slid her other hand in the v of his Levi's, sliding her hand to wrap around his balls. He tightened at the smoothness of her fingers surrounding his sensitive sacs. Her thumb slowly caressed them. He shuddered.

"So soft," Connie whispered.

She leaned forward and engulfed him in her mouth. He exhaled at the smooth wet warmth encasing him, groaning as she started to suck. Her tongue added to the sensations as she bobbed up and down his shaft.

Kai quickly pulled over to the side of the road. Connie, too intent on her prize, didn't even seem to notice. Kai spread his legs as much as he could in the close confines of the cab. He slid one hand down Connie's back, needing the contact with her. Sliding it past the waistband, caressing the soft skin of the small of her back. She wiggled and sucked harder. Pressure built inside him.

He grabbed Connie's head and arched up, forcing her to take him deeper. She hummed in appreciation and squeezed his balls. The globes tightened as she continued to suck. The soft, moist walls of her mouth and the teasing pressure of her teeth as she scraped along his length tantalizing him to the edge of bursting, his cock aching to cum. Kai held her head down exploding into her mouth, jerking as stream after stream erupted from him. Connie sucked and continued to rub his sensitive skin. He jerked from the sensation.

"No more, sweets."

Connie peeked up at him pulling away, the hot swipe of her tongue involuntarily clenching his groin. The warmth of her mouth replaced by the cool air in the truck. Smiling as she made him shudder, Connie caressed his balls and pulled her soft fingers away.

"Thank you." His voice was hoarse.

She sat up smiling and licking her lips. "I couldn't resist." Connie smiled, her eyes sparkling. "Don't you think we should head home?" She looked around sitting up. "Why did you stop?"

"You'd rather we drove off the road?"

Connie laughed. "No, of course not."

"Then I had to stop." He could devour her right now. Sated or not, he would always want her. Having found his mate, it was hard not to claim her immediately. He waited so long. No matter how hard Connie fought the pull, she was his mate. He would persuade her. "Come here." Kai reached for her.

"Oh no." Connie slid against the opposite door. "We need to get home."

Kai flashed a grin, reaching for her. "You weren't worrying about that a moment ago."

Connie giggled, her eyes sparkling. "No, I want to go home now." She grabbed the door handle as he tried to pull her over. "Kai, why don't we head home?"

Kai smiled. Connie's giggles filled the air with joy. Her happy face and the flush of arousal that tinted her cheeks pink made him want to pull her into his arms.

"Fine, but when we get there…"

"Ya, ya, ya."

He chuckled, her sassiness and ease around him made him feel whole and happy. No doubt she was the one for him. He ruffled her hair, adoring her outraged squeak, and shifted the truck back into drive, checking the mirror before pulling into the road.

"Put your seat belt on."

"Okay." Connie snuggled back into his side.

He heard the soft click of the belt connecting. Her weight settled against him, fitting like the final piece of a puzzle. They drove home, the road slightly bumpy from the patchwork done on it since winter. It was either winter or road repair. Kai could feel the acrid burn of the asphalt in his nose as they drove. His lust partially sated, he glanced back, the feeling bothering him all day still there, though diminished. No one followed them and despite Connie's delightful surprise blow job, he'd kept an eye out.

"Why do you keep looking back?" She glanced into the rear view mirror. "No one is following us."

"I know. I was just uneasy all day."

"Hmm, well, we're almost back at Ellen's and we're okay. I think we can relax now."

"Yes. The farm is wired to keep you protected and should give warning of any trespassers." Out of the corner of his eye he could see her shake her head. "What?"

"I just think this is being blown out of proportion. Who is going to bother to drive up here to get me?"

Kai held in his frustration. He knew Connie felt more and more comfortable. He also knew being here made the danger seem unreal to her. He'd called her brother while she worked today. Ellen texted the number when he'd asked for it. Just to get a better feel for the situation. However, he worried more after the call.

According to her brother, the last thing the dealer wanted was to go to jail for murder. It was much easier to kill Connie, thus eliminating the only witness to the crime.

Kai frowned. He would have to keep an eye out. He checked the mirror again. Nothing back there. He hoped it stayed that way. He pulled Connie tighter to him. She just smiled and rubbed her cheek against him. There was more her brother wasn't telling him. Kai could hear it in his voice when he'd called. He'd bet the danger was more imminent than expected.

Kai turned, heading into the driveway. He pulled up to the barn and parked. Unsnapping the seat belts, he turned and quickly flipped Connie to her back, stretching to lay over her. She giggled again.

Kai ran his nose up her neck, kissing and licking, nipping at her ear. Enjoying her moans with each caress. His body on fire from the scent and taste of her.

"We're here. Now, I can eat you up." Connie squirmed against him, her laughter and halfhearted attempts to escape just inflaming him further. She held onto his back, sliding a hand down to grasp his ass.

"Mmm."

She wiggled until he settled into the v of her body, his hardness cushioned by the soft warm cradle. He ground into her, hearing her gasp. Her hands roamed, trying to caress him through the heavy denim he wore. He laughed at her grunt. She tried to wiggle her fingers into the waistband of his pants.

"Haven't you been in there enough today?" He smiled at her and nipped her nose. "Why don't we take care of this in the house?" He felt her pinch his side in retaliation. "Hey now, no cause for that." He grinned down at her and sat up, pulling her with him. "Time to go in."

She shook her head. "Fine. I'm hungry anyway." Connie pushed at him, trying to get him to move from the truck. "Move."

Kai smiled and got out. Reaching back in, he pulled Connie out, plastering her to his front, trapping her between him and the seat. "There's no escape, Connie." He knew she was just thinking of now, but he meant it. There would be no escape from him. However, now that he'd found her he could make sure she was happy with him. He lowered his head, nibbling at the softness of her lips, enjoying the minty taste of her mouth as his tongue swiped along the seams, gently parting her lips for a deeper foray. He groaned, their tongues dueling, her flavor an aphrodisiac.

A sharp knock on the hood and he looked up into Maxwell's laughing face. "Get a room, old man." Connie squeaked and buried her face into his chest. It didn't help matters that the heat between her legs made him ache to slide inside. Her breasts, firm and peaked, pressed into his chest as she hid her face. He couldn't tell if she was embarrassed or laughing. She surprised him at every turn. One minute, a woman in all her glory, the next a giggling little girl.

Her arms tightened around him, eliciting a groan from him. Whatever she was, her body was all woman, and he wanted to savor that. Kai stepped back, letting Connie slide to the ground before he took her right there on the truck seat for all the world to watch. He could care less, but Connie definitely would. The night in the pond proved that.

"If you don't want to be stripped right here, proving you're mine, we need to get inside."

Connie laughed, flushing even pinker. "I don't think so, mister." Pushing him away, she turned and sashayed toward the house. Glancing over her shoulder, she winked. "What are you waiting for?"

Kai strode forward, swung her into his arms and headed inside.

Maxwell watched, their combined laughter echoing behind them. No one saw the silent watcher, the glint of the sun on the binoculars the only hint that they were under observation.

CHAPTER THIRTEEN

Connie sighed, the warm water running down her back. Her muscles relaxed, the beating of the massage setting kneading her already sated muscles. She turned and gasped, the warm streams of water abrading her sensitive nipples. They were slightly sore, the water stinging from Kai's attentions. She turned and let the soothing water massage her shoulders. Grabbing a wash puff, she added soap and lathered up. The soft scrape of the puff against her skin energizing, the scent of the soap refreshing.

Quickly rinsing off, Connie watched the bubbles go down the drain. Turning off the water, she stepped out and grabbed a towel. The rough texture against her skin absorbing the water. Wrapping it around herself, Connie tucked the ends in to hold it on and returned to her bedroom. She smiled at the rumpled bed.

Kai was definitely growing on her. His touch sent zings through her system. Just being near him sent shivers over her skin. Her resistance was failing. Connie laughed. Hell, what resistance? She started this latest round.

Plopping down on the bed, she stared at the wall, thinking about Kai. She really liked him. He was everything she wanted in a man. Strong, protective, maybe even a little too protective, and he treated her like gold. She smiled, liking the thought of being considered precious. His arrogance, however, was not an attractive trait, but one she feared was ingrained in him.

Connie wondered just how old Kai was. He didn't look a day over thirty, but if he was a friend of her grandfather's, he had to be really old. Grandpa was. She scrunched her nose at the thought. Maybe she didn't want to know.

Shifters lived really long lives. Needing to finish school was probably a drop in the bucket to the length of Kai's life; more mature than the young men she usually dated. Probably that age thing again.

She could hear noises from the kitchen. She fell asleep wrapped in his arms only to wake to find Kai gone. His scent still on her pillow. The evidence of his touch obvious in the tenderness of her skin. Connie stretched and stood, the towel dropping to the floor. Hearing more activity she knew dinner would be done soon and she needed to help Ellen. Opening the dresser she slid on a pair of lace panties. Opening another drawer, she grabbed a pair of shorts and a cami with a built-in bra. Sliding them on, she quickly wrapped her hair carelessly in a ponytail, opened the door and headed into the kitchen.

Stepping into the room, she laughed. Ellen was sitting at the table eating chocolate chip cookie dough.

"No dinner?"

Ellen looked up. "Nope." She smiled. "I think

we're going to have pizza. I have a few frozen ones in the freezer and I don't feel like cooking. Would you mind fixing them?"

"Not at all. We can't have you over doing it now that we know you're pregnant with triplets."

Ellen laughed. "How far do you think I can use that?"

Connie shook her head and opened the freezer. Looking in, she grabbed four pizzas. "Probably through the rest of your pregnancy." She lifted a brow at Ellen. "At least with Breccan and Maxwell."

The girls looked at each other and snickered.

Connie would enjoy the coming months. Ellen would have Breccan jumping through hoops. Poor guy. She could just imagine Kai doing the same. Connie groaned. He had her brain waves scrambled. That is the last thing she should be picturing. Connie checked the directions on the pizzas, went over and turned on the oven. Time to think of something, anything else.

"So, where did the guys go?"

"They were checking over the security footage from the cameras. Do you think they're taking it too far?"

Ellen shoved in another mouthful of cookie dough.

"I really don't know, Ellen." She leaned back against the counter. "But I suppose better safe than sorry." Her arm was getting tingly. Looking down, she realized she still held the pizza on her arm and turned around and slid it into the oven. "Nothing's happened, but it really hasn't been that long. Hopefully, nothing will happen."

"I hope nothing does." Ellen pulled the spoon out of her mouth. "If something does, they'll never let us forget it."

"You're right about that. They don't seem like the type to forget easily."

Ellen nodded her head in agreement. "They don't."

Connie finished getting the pizzas in. Luckily, Ellen had a double oven and they could cook two pizzas at once in each one. Finished putting them in, Connie sat across from Ellen.

"So, were you going to make cookies?"

Ellen smirked. "I was, but then I tasted the batter and couldn't wait."

"Well, I could put the rest of it on a cookie tray,"

offered Connie.

Ellen looked down at the cookie dough and at her hand holding the spoon. "I suppose," Ellen grumbled.

Connie grinned. She could tell Ellen didn't really want to give up her treat. "I'm sure Breccan and Maxwell would like some cookies."

Ellen stuck her tongue out at her.

"I'm sure you want cookies too, don't you?"

She grabbed the batter, pulling it to her. "I don't feel like sharing. Call it a craving." She smirked.

Connie snorted, rolling her eyes. "You're a brat."

"You love me anyway."

"True." Connie leaned closer to Ellen. "Have I gotten any mail yet?"

"You mean like from a school?" Ellen's eyes widened in mock surprise.

"Funny. Have I?"

"No." Ellen dug back into the cookie dough.

Connie sat back, disappointment rushing through her. She didn't know what she'd do if she didn't get accepted into UW. She gnawed her lip. She didn't relish the idea of going back to Chicago and running into any of the gang she'd seen. She knew from listening to her brother's horror stories, gangs were a problem in Chicago. Seeing the violence first hand shook her up. No matter what the police did, the gangs continued. She was scared to go home. She didn't want to admit it, though. She didn't know if their reach encompassed Wisconsin, she hoped not. Connie worried the situation was as dire as the men were treating it. But prayed it was a longshot.

"I'll let you know right away if you do, though." Ellen popped another spoonful of dough into her mouth.

"Thanks. Do you really think they'll accept me?" Connie tapped her fingers against the counter. The repetitive sound soothed her.

"Why wouldn't they?"

"It's past the application date."

Ellen made a rude noise. "They'd be lucky to have you. Think positive."

"Yeah, I will." Connie sat down and looked around the room. She'd love to have a kitchen like this. Ellen redid it beautifully, a classic look to fit the style of the house. She peeked at the timer, her tummy rumbling. The pizzas still not done. "Do you think the men have a reason to take all of these precautions? I don't think they're coming after me. What would be the point?" Connie knew she was repeating herself, but she couldn't help worrying. The precautions just made her jumpy.

"Better safe than sorry. Believe me, I know." Ellen's voice lowered. "I would hate to have you go through what I did."

Connie looked at her and squeezed her eyes shut. She hated what happened to Ellen. At least she knew she was being hunted. "I guess you're right."

The oven buzzed and Connie jumped out of the chair, opening the oven to check out the pizzas. "They look good. Should I put in a couple more for the guys?"

"Definitely, they'll probably eat a whole one each. Three more pizzas should do it."

"Um, Ellen, I already have four made."

Ellen raised a brow.

"So? I'm eating for four here."

Connie looked at her, startled and began to laugh. "So you're not willing to share? Fine. I'll put four more in then. Just so you know, I'm not eating a whole pizza by myself."

"Don't worry, it won't go to waste."

Connie shook her head, laughing. She pulled the pizzas from the oven and put two of them in the warming tray and two on the table. She grabbed more from the freezer and put them in the oven, and sat back down.

"Ellen, what's it like being mated to a shifter? Really. Do they do anything weird? Stuff I might not know about? Do they know you when they're shifted or are they really just animals then? Do they ever bite? Do they sleep in bed as wolves or men? Do they ever get frisky in wolf form?"

Ellen looked at her, mouth open and then started laughing.

"Oh, my God! Really?"

Connie pouted. She needed to know and here Ellen was laughing at her. Sleeping with wolves would be like sleeping with dogs, but she couldn't imagine sleeping with a dragon would be at all comfortable.

"Who else can I ask?"

Ellen snickered and finally stopped.

"They are just as weird as normal men. Of course they know me when they're wolves. Remember? They followed me everywhere before they let me know they were shifters. They have a lot of animal instincts, but they have them no matter the shape they're in. They can bite. I understand each type of shifter has their own mating rituals. Breccan and Maxwell are wolves. Kai isn't of course." Ellen looked at her and laughed. "If they slept in the bed as wolves, I wouldn't have a bed left, they're too big." Ellen blushed and cleared her throat. "For the last? I plead the fifth!"

"What do you mean mating rituals? I thought you were either mates or you weren't?" God, what if Kai needed to bite her in dragon form? He'd swallow her in one bite.

"There is a binding ritual. It will tie you together for life. Even I knew that before I mated."

Connie definitely needed to talk to Kai. "Pardon me for growing up in the city. It's not like there were a lot of shifters there. I thought most of them preferred the country life so they could let their animals free."

"They're everywhere from what I understand. Do you have any more questions?"

"Hmm. I'm sure I'll come up with more, but that's

good for now." The oven dinged. Connie stood up. "I'll get these out and call in the men."

Ellen pushed back from the table and stood up. "I'll put away the cookie dough." She grabbed the bowl, put plastic wrap over the top, and slid it into the fridge. "Oh, would you like a salad with the pizza? I can make one up real quick."

"Sounds good." Connie pulled out the pizzas and turned the ovens off. She headed to the door and stuck out her head. She didn't see any of the men, so she rang the triangle Ellen installed on the porch.

Connie came back inside. Sniffing, her tummy rumbled. Maybe she could eat a whole pizza.

Ellen tossed the salad and set it in the center of the table. She finished by adding a few more ingredients. Ellen grabbed plates and forks from the cabinet and stacked them next to the salad.

Connie sliced the pizzas and placed as many as she could on the table.

The three men arrived talking and laughing and headed to the sink to wash. Connie's breath caught. She watched Kai move across the room. His grace emphasizing the power in his body. Breccan swooped in to kiss Ellen as Kai grabbed Connie and pulled her close to do the same. She threw her arms around his neck. He made her feel safe. Even the churning in her stomach stopped.

"Mmm, dinner smells great." Kai nuzzled her ear.

"It's just salad and pizza." Connie gasped.

"It will do fine."

Connie shivered, the deep rumble of Kai's voice against her neck making her wish they were alone. *Maybe*, she thought, *maybe there is something to this mate business after all.*

****

Kai loved the shiver that snaked down Connie's spine. His nostrils flared as he breathed in the scent of her skin, the slight smell of her perspiration and the unmistakable trace of her arousal. His arms slid across soft skin as he pulled her close, wrapping her in his arms.

"Mate," he rumbled, enjoying the feel of her curves against him. She turned her head and smiled up at him. His heart stuttered. Maybe she was done fighting the truth. That she was his.

Elbows poked him in the stomach. Connie wriggled free from his arms. His muscles loosened, letting her go.

"Time to eat." Connie slid in a chair.

Kai loved her breathlessness. His chest swelled. He did that. Kai leaned down to place a soft kiss on her cheek, sitting next to her. Despite the joy Connie brought him, uneasiness still rode him. Something was coming this way. He could feel it. Kai decided he would continue to drive Connie to work each day and pick her up. Breccan and Maxwell were just going to have to start picking up the pace to take over the work on the farm.

Kai knew he would be gone sooner rather than later now he'd found his mate. He had zero intentions of living at Ellen's once he mated Connie. He gritted his teeth. He could barely reign in his dragon. He wouldn't complete the mating without Connie's permission. He could, if he wanted his mate pissed at him forever, but he wouldn't. He glanced at his mate, his gaze softening. Connie was worth waiting for. Kai gained patience over the centuries. It was finally time to exercise it. He stood and checked the windows again before sitting and pulling Connie closer.

She smiled up at him. "Eat. We didn't slave over a hot oven to put this feast in front of you for you to turn your nose up at it."

Kai snorted and raised a brow at her, trying to reign in his amusement.

"Slaved, over pizza? I can assume you made the crust from scratch and carefully put only the freshest ingredients on it, just for me." He lightly kissed her nose. He loved when Connie teased him.

Connie giggled. "Well, I cooked them at any rate."

"And I made the salad," Ellen piped in.

"Bagged, I assume?" Breccan added drily.

The women looked at each other and laughed.

"At least we're feeding you." Ellen flicked a piece of sausage at Breccan who snapped it out of the air.

"Don't waste the good bits!" Breccan's smile was full of teeth. Kai could see he shifted just a bit for effect. He shook his head. Sometimes the antics of the wolves made him feel every century his age. The giggling of his mate reversed that. She made him feel young again, made him feel alive.

"Silly wolves." His whisper in Connie's ear turned her to him.

She reached up and kissed his jawline, lightly scratching by his ear. "They're entertaining. Perfect for Ellen, she needs the joy they bring."

"They've brought her bundles of joy for sure. The coming months will be interesting."

Connie choked on a laugh. "Kai!"

Kai grinned down, the sight of the laughter on her face, her eyes sparkling made his heart beat faster. He hugged her to him, before releasing her to grab another slice of pizza.

The conversation turned, centering on the expected babies and the wedding happening sooner rather than later. Dinner complete, they all moved into the living room. Breccan snuggled on the couch with Ellen. Kai pulled Connie into his lap in the oversized arm chair, definitely a piece of furniture made for snuggling. Maxwell rolled his eyes at all of them and turned on the television, ignoring the giggles and whispers.

Soon, they were all laughing at a sitcom on TV. Connie's curves against him all warm and soft, soon gave rise to an ache in his groin. Kai couldn't help his reaction. His dragon wanted nothing more than to sink into her warmth and wallow there. He tightened his arms around her, his body on fire, but content to have her safe in his arms.

Connie squirmed in his lap as she began kissing him on the neck. He groaned at the soft kisses. Her breath making him erect in anticipation, his groin throbbing in hot desperation.

"Don't you like it?" Connie whispered in his ear and nibbled on his lobe.

He groaned. Kai could feel the hard tips of her nipples against his arm and chest. He knew damn well she hadn't put a bra on. He became aware of it at dinner.

"Yes." To all of it dammit. He liked her pressing against him. He liked her nibbling on his ear. He liked the feel of her breasts against him. He liked the tempting warmth of her body squirming on his. He slid a hand up, skimming the side of her leg and slid beneath her shorts, curving her tempting ass. He groaned when he encountered her panties. He slid his long fingers further, touching the wet heat of her center, teasing her through the lace that prevented him from sinking into his goal and stealing her control.

"Kai..." Connie sighed, spreading her legs just a bit. Kai shifted, his fingers gaining room to pet more of her. The rise of her hips to his touch sent a shaft of satisfaction to his soul. Connie could protest all she wanted, but his dragon recognized her soul and she was his. One way or another, she would acknowledge she was his mate, but for now, he'd enjoy her moans.

"Are you ready for bed? You have to work in the morning, don't you?" Kai ground out. It was time for bed, not that he planned to sleep.

"Yes. I have to be there at eight."

Kai stood, swinging Connie into his arms. Breccan's eyes caught the movement and looked over.

"Going to bed?"

"Yes." Kai nodded. He smiled and nodded toward Ellen. "Looks like little momma there is already in dreamland."

"I don't want to disturb her yet. She's been sick,

though she was trying to hide it. At least we know why now."

"That's good. Don't leave her like that too long. It'll probably give her a stiff neck."

"I know. When she's a bit deeper asleep, I'll move her to bed. Have a good night." Breccan's snicker had Kai's eyes narrowing.

"Make sure the doors are locked and the alarm set." He wanted Connie more than a fight with the wolf. Kai needed to remember how young the wolves were.

"Maxwell will make a final run through before we go to bed."

"Good night." Kai nodded and headed off to Connie's room. It was time to explore his mate and give a little payback for the teasing this evening. Glancing down into Connie's eyes, the telltale blush creeping up her chest and blossoming on her cheeks, showed her arousal. The spicy scent emanating from her told him his mate would not be refusing his attentions tonight. His heart beat in anticipation as he strode down the hall with the heated bundle in his arms.

No one noticed the shadows creeping around

outside. The cameras wouldn't show anything amiss as the shadows hid in the darkness they were used to.

CHAPTER FOURTEEN

Another day at the office. Connie put away supplies. Earlier she'd given routine vaccinations under Aiden's watchful eye. She was okay with that. She knew she would have to prove herself.

An interesting day either way. She didn't realized the main exotic pet care Aidan did was on shifters. She'd also found out not only was he a doctor of veterinary medicine, but also, a regular people doctor. He combined the two to treat both sides of a shifter. Connie couldn't help admiring him. She finished with the supplies and skipped to check in with Lou and see where she might be needed.

"I'm done with the supplies. What else can I do?" She couldn't keep the smile off her face. Last night Kai showed her another side to him, tenderness in every touch.

"Aidan said to have you head back to exam room one. The chart is on the wall." Lou picked up the ringing phone. "Animal Kingdom, Lou speaking. How may I help you?"

Connie turned and headed to the exam room. She assumed it was a routine exam. Knocking and then entering, she read the file. A pregnant kitty in for a routine exam, but from the chart, this kitty visited quite a few times. Connie wondered if she was having any problems not listed.

"Oh! Who are you?"

Connie looked up at the speaker. In front of her was a tall blonde, dressed to the nines. Connie felt drab in her scrubs by comparison.

"Hi, I'm Connie. I'm the new veterinary tech

here." She smiled and reached toward the pet cage the woman was holding. "Here, let's let her out."

"I always see Dr. Aidan. Where is he?"

"He's seeing another patient. He assigned me your case." Connie didn't much care for snotty patrons, but she did care about the pets.

"Well, I never. Fine, you can look at Fluffy, but be very careful."

"I'll just take her cage and put it up here to open it." Connie took the cage as she spoke and then gently opened the door. A plaintive meow preceded the cat from the cage. "Oh, she's adorable."

"Thank you."

Connie could detect a thaw in the woman's voice as she oohed over the exotic shorthair when she stretched and strolled out of the cage like a mini queen.

"I just prefer to make sure her pregnancy is going well."

Connie looked at the chart and examined the snow white cat in front of her. Fluffy let Connie do the examination, purring as her hands checked her over.

"She appears to be doing just fine. She should be

having her kittens within the week. She's healthy and well fed. It looks like you do a wonderful job of taking care of her."

The woman preened. Connie stifled a laugh, the owner reminding her of the cat she examined.

"Thank you. I try to take care of Fluffy as well as I can."

"It shows. She shouldn't have any trouble having her kittens. You can contact us if there is any problem." Connie petted Fluffy before gently placing her back in her cage. "Do you have any questions?"

"What do I do if Fluffy has her kittens after hours?"

"There is an emergency line that will contact either Dr. Aidan or one of the vet techs if you have any problems."

"Okay. Thank you for checking out Fluffy."

"You're welcome. Here you go. Remember, if you have any problems, give us a call. You can check out with Lou in the front."

"I will. Thank you."

The woman headed toward the counter and Connie

followed, jotting down notes and handing it over to Lou. He nodded, smiled and turned to the counter to enter the information into the computer.

"Now, Miss Harlow, your cost for today's exam is fifty dollars." He handed her the bill. "Do you want to pay it now or shall we bill you?"

"I'll pay it now, of course."

Distracted by the phone, Connie picked it up while Lou finished with the Harlow cat. The rest of the day followed the same pattern, routine pet exams and answering the phone.

A thrill of excitement ran down her spine, at a final tinkle of the bell on the door. Kai was here. She didn't even have to see him to know it. Her body's response told her.

"Kai, what are you doing here?" Connie heard the teasing in Aidan's voice. "Do you need an exam? Getting too old to get it up? I have just the prescription for you."

Connie giggled at Kai's growl.

"Shut up." The exasperation in Kai's voice clear. "You know I'm here to pick up my mate."

Connie rolled her eyes before heading toward the

front.

"No one here is marked, so I've no idea who you mean." Aiden raised his brows, looking around the room before turning back to his brother.

Kai growled and grabbed his brother, who grinned like a loon.

"Kai!" Connie stepped forward and placed her hand on his arm. "Don't go getting me fired."

"Yeah, Kai, listen to the unmarked woman here." His egging of Kai tempted Connie to smack Aiden, but she worried it would cost her the job she needed.

Kai growled and pushed him away.

"Our dam wouldn't be happy if I got rid of you anyway." He slipped his arm around Connie's waist and pulled her close to him. "Time to go."

"Night, Dr. Aidan."

"Goodnight, Connie. I'll see you tomorrow." He waved them off, a big grin on his face.

"Night, Connie." The phone rang, Lou waved goodbye and answered it.

"Night, Lou."

"Enough." Kai practically dragged her out of the

office. "Time to go."

Watching the tic in his jaw, she dug her heals in. Her feelings for Kai were all mixed up, but she wasn't ready to let him dictate to her. Time to stop it before he got worse.

"Kai, quit dragging me around. What is the matter with you?"

He growled. That wasn't the answer she was looking for.

"Kai?"

He stopped. Digging her heals in hadn't really helped. Connie knew he could have continued if he'd wanted. He listened, not very happily, but he did.

"What?"

"What is the matter with you?" Connie didn't know whether to be exasperated or flattered over his obvious jealousy.

Kai stood there, aggravation written plainly on his face. His jaw clenched.

"Did I do something wrong?"

"No," Kai grumbled grudgingly. "You did nothing wrong." He ran a hand through his hair and pulled her into his arms. "You smell like Aidan, and that pup. You'd smell like me if we were mated."

Yup, she was going with exasperation. Connie shook her head. She wasn't sure she could choose between Kai and becoming a veterinarian. She needed to make sure Kai understood and accepted her goals. Her stomach clenched. She didn't know what she would do if he didn't. The discussion absolutely necessary for her peace of mind. Her heart raced, worrying everything in her grasp could be taken away.

"I'm not ready." If only he understood that. Connie bit her lip. She didn't think he did.

"I know. I'm giving you time. I don't want to but, I will." Kai pulled her into his arms. His voice rough. "We need to go."

She burrowed into his chest. His arms around her made her feel safe, warm and cherished. Connie hugged him tighter.

"We really need to go." Kai loosened his embrace.

"Okay, but why are you so insistent?"

"Something doesn't feel right. I sense a threat. It might be nothing, but I've lived long enough to trust my instincts. We need to go."

"Do you think your brother is in trouble?"

"He's always in trouble." The grin Kai flashed sent heat rushing through her veins. Connie could feel her nipples tighten and her panties dampen. "But no, I know it centers on you. I think we need to be careful. Maybe alert the police."

"We can't just say your instincts tell you I'm in danger."

"Why not?" Kai urged her toward the vehicle. "Let's go home."

Connie nodded, looking forward to going home too. She scurried to the truck, thinking of being watched unnerving her. Knowing someone might be hunting her made her feel that way. She just might have to start carrying her gun. It was small enough to carry easily in an ankle holster, but how awkward would that be if she needed it? Maybe she'd go online and see what other types of holsters there were.

Her brother insisted she learn. The perks of him being a cop. Nervous at first, she found she enjoyed it. She'd never wanted to hunt, but she enjoyed target practice, admitted to herself carrying her Sig Sauer made her feel safe. It was small enough for her to conceal and powerful enough to do the job. Luckily, the concealed carry classes in Illinois were so stringent that most of the surrounding states accepted the Illinois permit, so she was legal in case of any issues.

Connie slid in the seat and watched as Kai closed her door and looked around. His features sharper than normal. She could see his dragon looking out. She shivered, that glimpse made her realize Kai was by no means tame.

****

Kai felt his senses heighten. His dragon on edge. The air seemed to quiver with something, someone unknown. His first instinct to protect his mate. They were going home. He would prefer his cave, but Connie wouldn't approve.

Time enough to share that when they mated. In her dragon form, the intricate and intertwined caverns would fascinate her. He hoped. Glancing around again, Kai climbed in and pulled Connie toward him.

She slid easily over, snuggling into him and snapping her seatbelt into place.

He turned the key in the ignition, the smooth purr of the engine signaled the beginning of their drive home. Kai reversed the truck, glancing over his shoulder. He stopped at Connie's words.

"Kai, you have to wear your belt, too." Connie reached over him and pulled the strap across his chest, snapping it in place. "It's the law."

"I wouldn't get hurt." His chest warmed at Connie's concern. She could deny him all she wanted, but her actions told a different story. She was his mate.

"So you say. It's still the law and I'd rather get home than sit at the side of the road while you get a ticket."

Kai snorted and continued out of the parking stall. Ignoring the scent of his mate and concentrating on driving. He needed to stay alert. Certain someone watched. Connie's enemies at hand, ignorant of what they were facing. His dragon rose. Kai clenched his fists on the steering wheel. Shifting in the truck would harm his mate. If he could, he would wrap her up and hide her away for centuries. He'd found his treasure and they wouldn't get a chance to take her away.

His radio crackled on. Connie fiddling with the channels.

"What are you doing?" Kai winced. He would prefer the radio off, but indulging Connie came naturally.

"I feel like listening to some music."

He snorted. He got one, maybe two channels at most, country or old rock. On Sundays both gospel. He didn't listen much on Sundays. He'd never made up his mind about the human's god. Dragons never gave how or why they were created much thought. There since the beginning was how dragon lore told it.

He smiled, Connie settling on a station. She began to hum and attempt to sing along.

"Happiness...um, um. 'Cause I'm happy, uh huh, um, um."

Kai snorted, choking on a laugh. Connie couldn't remember the words to the song and she couldn't carry a tune. She was happy though, a grin on her face, be-bopping along to the music.

Kai glanced in the mirror. The road to the farm, though not well-travelled did see traffic. A dark blue sedan trailed behind him. It set the nape of his neck to itching. Nothing showed the car behind him a threat, but somehow, some way, he knew. If Connie wasn't with him he'd take care of it. Nothing would stop his dragon from eliminating the threat. But her safety came first. His chest rumbled quietly, his dragon preparing to remove the threat.

Kai turned into the drive, keeping an eye on the car behind him. It wasn't so close he could see who was behind the wheel. The car's speed continued unabated, driving past their turn. Kai frowned. Maybe he was seeing threats where there were none. He drove down the gravel drive, keeping a watch in the rear view mirror and trying to expand his senses to the utmost. The threat niggled at the corner of his consciousness. Not enough for him to pinpoint and eliminate it.

"We're here. Are you going to stop or drive

straight into the garage? It would help if you opened the door first."

Kai slammed on the brakes. Connie jerked forward in exaggeration.

"Jeez, pay attention much?" Connie disengaged her belt and turned to him. "Kai, what's the matter?" She unhooked his as she slid her arms around him. "Hmm?"

He pulled her in close, loving the feeling of her curves against him. His cock jumped as she snuggled close, the tip of her tongue flickering against the edge of his jaw.

"Trouble is coming," he growled, a shiver racing up his spine. The heat of her tongue arousing him. "I'd say it's already here." Kai turned, shifting her faster than she could blink, and pulling her under him. Done with her teasing, he flicked open his Levi's and pulled down her scrub pants, shoving aside the thong she barely wore and sliding into her wet depths. He groaned. So hot and wet, he knew she would be ready for him.

"Kai," Connie moaned.

He pounded into her. Wanting to imprint himself. The shift of her breasts teased him. He wanted nothing more than to strip her bare. Shoving up her scrub top and bra, Kai caught his breath. Her breasts bounced with each of his thrusts, tempting him. Her hard, ripe nipples teased him until he bent and latched on, suckling as he fucked her. She squeezed around him, strangling him as he sucked harder. So wet, Kai slid easily in her juices. His back tingled and balls tightened. Sliding a finger down to her clit, Kai flicked it. Connie came with a wail. Kai gritted his teeth, pounding her depth, shooting his warmth into her. It was all he could do not to make her his at that moment.

His dragon wanted her, desired her and demanded he keep her safe. He knew she would be if she became his. He wouldn't worry about her survival if she became his mate. The dragon inside her would protect her.

"Mate me?" A moan was his only reply. His chest swelled at the glow on her body, the satiated look on her face.

"I can't."

Coldness spread from his heart. Kai withdrew, sliding out of her warmth and the truck. He stood, staring at her. He needed to understand why. He knew Connie was his. She was putty in his hands. At least, in everything but this.

"Why not?" A sigh was his answer. Connie sat up, pulling her bra and top down with a curse as she struggled to pull it over her breasts. Kai eyed her, enjoying the pink tipped treats as they disappeared from view.

"I just can't. I'm waiting."

"Waiting for what? You are my mate. Why should we wait?" Connie's nostrils flared, Kai knew the impatience he felt was evident in his voice just by the look on her face.

"Move. Out of my way." Connie scrambled to get her bottoms on as she slid across the seat. "I don't have to explain myself. You don't own me." She pushed him aside, grabbing her pants and sliding them on. "When I'm ready, I'll let you know. With your attitude, it will be a good long while." She snapped the elastic of her pants, adjusting them around her tiny waist. Even that sounded pissed.

Kai ground his teeth and stepped back. Not sure exactly why she was in a snit. He should be. He knew and she knew, she belonged to him. Denying him wouldn't last forever.

Connie was a bit secretive lately, but that could have something to do with the wedding Ellen and she were planning. He truly wasn't pushing as hard as he could be. He'd have to let her come to him. Dragon's just weren't patient, especially fire dragons like him. It would be hard, but worth it in the end. Their passions ran as hot as the flames running through them. If Kai changed Connie and she was pissed, he wasn't sure he'd want to face her. Which would defeat the purpose of having her as his mate. Maybe. He loved her temper.

Kai's eyes followed her to the house. Despite everything, Kai wanted her under him despite the danger closing in. If he didn't change her before the danger arrived and she was injured or killed, he would never forgive himself. But he couldn't force the mating on her, Connie had to submit of her own free will.

CHAPTER FIFTEEN

Connie knew she was being unreasonable. She stomped up the steps to the porch. Kai wasn't asking anything she wasn't asking herself. She needed to sit down and talk with him. He just overwhelmed her sometimes. She was afraid if she told him about applying to UW it would somehow curse it. She just hoped she'd hear soon.

"Connie, you got mail." Ellen sounded excited as she handed it to her.

Connie looked at the address. It was from UW. Taking a deep breath, Connie opened it and started reading. She looked up at Ellen. Her stomach churned.

"Well? What does it say?"

"Ellen." Connie looked at her, trying to stay calm. *The Hell with it* she thought. "I got in!" She started jumping up and grabbed Ellen in a hug. "I got in! Oh, my God! I can't believe it!"

"I knew you would!" Ellen squeezed her so hard she could hardly draw air into her lungs.

"Ellen," she wheezed. "You're choking me girl." Connie breathed deep, her lungs filling with life giving air as Ellen's arms dropped.

"I'm so excited you're going to stay. You'll be here for my babies. I'll have my best friend close by." Ellen closed in and her arms enveloped Connie, surrounding her with joy. Their happiness vibrated in the air.

"I can't wait." Connie pulled back from Ellen's arms. She danced, wiggling back and forth. "Just remember I have to stay in Madison to go to school. I'll only be up on the weekends." She couldn't wait to tell

Kai. She wouldn't have to choose. She couldn't wait to tell Kai.

"That will be just awesome, Connie." They grinned at each other.

"It will, won't it?" Connie's heart filled with joy. "I need to go change, then I'll be back to help with supper."

Connie skipped to her room, letter still grasped in her hand. Her heart fluttered. Her world felt brighter. Maybe now she'd be able to see if a relationship with Kai would work. He touched her and she went up in flames. She couldn't say no if she tried. She pressed her hand to her stomach, trying to stop the fluttering.

There was so much more than sex to a relationship, and that's what she wanted, a relationship. She gave no thought about it until she watched Ellen with Breccan. Connie didn't just want to be a convenient outlet. She wanted the whole nine yards. She wanted what Ellen had. A man to be there for her, to worship the ground she walked on. A man to start a family with, but one who supported her dreams.

She wasn't sure Kai offered what she wanted.

Connie wasn't willing to give up her dream to become a veterinarian. Would he support it? Of course, she needed to ask him. She did him a disservice assuming he would squash her dreams. He knew she attended veterinary school. Knew she applied for an internship and even drove her there and back. Why was she so damn scared to tell him?

Kai knocked her socks off from the first. He'd been staying in the house since Connie told them about the murder she'd witnessed. His protectiveness drew her, but she worried she was clinging to him because of the situation. Or could it be because he was darn near irresistible?

Connie giggled. Kai *was* pretty darn irresistible. But was that enough basis to tie herself to him for the rest of her life? He overwhelmed her. She really needed to find out what being mated entailed. At least now she had options. She could go back to Chicago to finish school or she could transfer to UW.

It wasn't that far to visit from UW. It was a lot closer to Kai and Ellen. Connie missed Ellen something fierce. Almost inseparable as children, becoming adults hardly changed a thing. Coming back here felt right, like home. Staying in Chicago would keep her near her parents and brothers, but the thought of going back there turned her stomach. Not to mention, the thought of leaving Kai caused her heart to clench and made her eyes sting.

"You coming out for dinner?" Ellen stuck her head in the door. "Or are you going to take a nap?"

"You're the only one taking naps. I was just thinking." Connie rolled off the bed, standing up.

"Well, get changed and come back to the kitchen." Ellen turned her head toward the kitchen and sniffed. "Dinner's almost done and the guys should be in soon." She closed the door and Connie could hear her heading down the hall.

She put the letter on the dresser, and stripped, heading to the shower. Before dinner, she needed to get clean. Working with animals all day may be her dream, but they stank. Connie appreciated being clean after a day of work. Not to mention the session with Kai in the truck.

She stepped in the shower. Connie filled her lungs,

the steam curling into her body with a deep breath. The muscles in her shoulders eased, the warmth flowing around her body. The needle sharp divots beating on her back forced groans from her. The tightness in her back easing under the spray. Standing there, warm and wet, Connie let her worries swirl and flow down the drain.

****

Kai reined in his aggravation. Connie wasn't ready. Making everything worse, Kai sensed the danger coming for her. The fact he couldn't mark her and give her the protection of her own dragon ate at him. He wanted to wrap his arms around her and never let her go. He wanted to stash her in his cave, safe and free from harm.

He hit his fist against the truck, an involuntary rumble slipping from his chest. He never imagined having a mate could tie him in knots.

"What did the truck do?" Breccan's amused voice came from behind him.

"Nothing."

"What did Connie do then?" Maxwell got to the heart of the matter.

"Nothing."

"Then what's the problem?" Breccan moved into his line of sight. Kai scowled at the grin on Breccan's face.

"How can I convince Connie to mate with me? You didn't have the problem I'm having."

Breccan shrugged. "It's a totally different situation. Connie doesn't feel she needs you to protect her. I don't think she really feels like she is in danger. Ellen needed me, needed us. I think Connie is a lot more independent."

"Connie needs me. Maybe she doesn't realize it, but something is coming this way. I can feel it in the air." Kai slammed the truck door shut. The scent of Connie's arousal permeated the air in the cab, ratcheting his senses and his frustrations.

Breccan and Maxwell nodded in agreement and looked around. The smiles dropped off their faces.

"We can feel it too." Breccan's features sharpened as he looked around. "It's coming. Evil has a scent to it and it's coming this way."

"If it's not already here." Kai's senses pinged, the blood rushing through his veins and his vision shifting. The dragon wanted out. "I'll keep watch tonight. I'll be on the roof once everyone goes to bed."

"I'll split the night with you. Maxwell, you can stay inside and protect Ellen and Connie. One of us should always be inside with them." Breccan nodded at Kai. "You can spend the second half with Connie."

Kai nodded in agreement. Having one of them inside would protect the women if somehow the house was breached.

"Make sure you set the alarms," Kai grunted. He knew they wouldn't forget, but couldn't help reminding them.

Nodding in agreement, they all headed toward the house.

Ellen stuck her head out the door and saw them approaching. "Good, I was just about to call you all in for supper."

Kai followed Breccan and Maxwell. His eyes centered on Connie placing the meal in the center of the table. Glancing from Connie to Ellen he could see the resemblance in their features. Connie's golden hair glowed in the light, a gift from her Scandinavian blood. Ellen's chestnut hair a gift from another ancestor. Connie's more outgoing personality called to him. He never liked guessing games and Connie's forthrightness appealed to him.

Despite the fact she refused to accept him as her mate yet, Kai knew it was only a matter of time. He snorted. He hoped. He hoped it was only a matter of time. She couldn't resist him, and he did everything he could to tempt her. Now that he found her, he fully intended on keeping her.

"Have a seat. Supper's ready." Ellen waved at the table.

Connie brought a pitcher of ice cold sweet tea to the table. She poured him a glass and blew in his ear. He couldn't hide his reaction, a shiver running down his spine. Connie stood back up with a giggle.

Kai reached for her and she skittered out of his way, filling each of the glasses around the table. "Connie."

She threw him a smile and set down the pitcher. "What?"

He couldn't help but smile. She no longer appeared aggravated with him and Kai decided to let it go.

"Sit down and eat." He patted the chair next to him.

Connie smiled, her face glowing and sat beside him. "I can do that." Her soft fingers trailed down his arm, soothing him. "We need to talk later."

The whisper low enough he didn't think anyone else at the table heard. He glanced at her and one look into her pleading blue eyes and he nodded. He would do anything for her. If Connie needed to talk, he would listen.

****

Fred watched the house from a distance. Jimmy back at the hotel room they shared. Fred knew enough to always have help handy. Jimmy the only one he trusted. Twins, they shared a bond that wouldn't allow betrayal.

Few knew the fact Jimmy and Fred were twins. They were rarely seen together. It was safer that way.

The security cameras were obvious if you knew what to look for and Fred did. Normally the houses they hit were unoccupied, at least other than their target. He needed to figure out a plan to get the girl away from the rest of the people in the house.

He didn't think he would be able to get to her here. Even if the cameras were a joke, there were just too many people around. It would be easier to target her at work. Fred knew he'd have to find out her schedule. So far it didn't seem she followed one, but he knew if he watched long enough he'd find it. Once he did, she would be his. No matter how long it took.

Maybe he'd be able to get both women. He'd enjoy that. The brunette would be a good appetizer to build his hunger up for blondie. He could picture her, tied up and helpless as he showed her just what he liked. The thought of her creamy skin marked and bleeding and the life leaving her eyes as he fucked her to death brought out a smile. Doing it with blondie watching, anticipating what he'd do to her, his balls tightened.

He managed to get close the other night. Listening at the windows jacking off. He marked each spot under the windows of the bedrooms, his seed burrowing in the ground. The sounds of nonstop sex excited him. He watched through the windows, imagining what he would do when it was his turn.

He wondered if they traded off or just enjoyed an orgy. Did the two women put on a show for the men? That would be hot. Maybe he would keep blondie alive for a bit and work off some of the edginess he carried around.

From the sounds, she would like it. He had skills, all the prostitutes told him so. He'd have her screaming for him before he was done. He could tell they liked it dirty, and he'd definitely give it to them.

Just thinking of it his balls tingled. Absentmindedly, he rubbed his erection through the gym pants he wore. Grunting, he grasped himself tighter, thrusting into his palm. He throbbed, the polyester was silky smooth against his skin as he pumped. A tingle ran from his balls down his cock. He tightened his hand. Thinking of the blonde, ramming into her, tits bouncing and screams coming from her throat as his hands tightened around her neck excited him. His dick jumped, spurting as he yanked down the elastic waist of his pants, watching a twisted stream of cum wasting away in the dirt at his feet.

Soon enough it would find a home. Absentmindedly he fondled himself, thinking of everything he would do to her.

Fred watched as the lights went off throughout the house and went on in what he knew were the bedrooms. They looked ready to settle in for the night. Fred thought about creeping closer, wanting to watch again, but decided against it. The lights stayed on and he thought about what was going on inside. His heart stuttered in excitement as his blood throbbed, rushing lower. He yanked, thrusting forward with each pull.

A thrum filled the air, tires on pavement. Fred stepped back behind the trees. A county police car drove by, slowing as he checked out the property. Apparently satisfied all was well, he gained speed again, moving off until the red of his taillights were no longer in view.

Fred chuckled. The cops wouldn't be able to stop

him. They never had before. Grabbing himself, he rubbed, just enough so that the tingles left a yearning ache in his cock. Nothing would stop him as he rode the blonde into hell.

There was a reason Fred was sent. The dick weed that blondie reported following her dispatched by Fred's hand for jeopardizing the bosses' safety. Without blondie, there was no evidence. Just an eye witness report. Soon enough they wouldn't have that, and the boss would be released.

The lights went off and Fred knew there would be no more movement for the night. He turned away. He didn't see the man leave the house. It was dark enough to hide the dragon as it flew to the roof to guard those inside. Fred moved off in the trees and headed back to his car. He'd have Jimmy contact the veterinarian in the morning for information, while he watched once again from the coffee shop. Soon enough he would have the girl at his mercy.

CHAPTER SIXTEEN

Connie headed into her bedroom. She wasn't sure what to say to Kai. Normally, she didn't have any problem making her feelings known. However, they overwhelmed her this time. Kai meant more to her than she'd ever thought possible, but he was so demanding. Connie could see this discussion going south before she figured out what to say.

Connie paced in front of the bed, the soft fibers of the carpet soothing against her feet. Her arms warm around her waist while she thought. The movement kept her focused. It was time to talk to Kai. The letter from UW arrived and exciting as it was, it was also terrifying. What would Kai think? Could they make this work?

She didn't want it to be just instinctual, him wanting her for a mate. Connie wanted Kai to have feelings for her. No doubt he wanted her. It showed in every touch. Hell, he touched her and she melted. Connie had absolutely no resistance to him what so ever and he knew it. Kai practically moved into her room. Rare he didn't spend the night with her since she arrived, all because she couldn't say no when he touched her.

The emotional stuff on the other hand she disregarded instinctively. But Ellen was right, she decided if she could see herself without Kai. But, did she want to see herself without him? Connie knew she didn't, but she also saw herself as a veterinarian. She always dreamed of becoming one.

Moving as a teenager pulled her away from the area and family she loved, away from the animals all around her. City life was fun, but it didn't satisfy her deep down in her soul. Now, Connie was where she belonged. Could Kai possibly be the reason? Connie closed her eyes, trying to imagine herself without Kai. She shivered, thinking of not knowing him. A gaping hole opened up in her heart, a bleakness that left her gasping. Connie held herself tightly and stood still, trembling at the pain the thought gave her. How could she give him up?

Connie feared what would happen if Kai disapproved of her dream. It was hers since she was a child. She loved animals. Could she give up her dream for Kai? Could she give up Kai for her dream? God, she hoped it she could have both.

"What's the matter?"

Connie warmed, strong arms sliding around her, stilling the shattering in her soul. She took a deep breath, the scent of musk and dirt and sweat settled in her lungs, calmed her trembling and spread a glow throughout her soul. Kai *was* home.

"Why are you crying?" A rough finger slid down her cheek, tracing a path she hadn't even realized was there.

"I was just thinking."

Kai sat on the bed, pulling Connie into his arms. His hard muscles held her steady, his arms encircled her, their strength sending shards of happiness through her. She was safe, every touch ensured her of that.

"Of what? What are you thinking that made you cry?"

"You."

"What?" Kai's outrage made Connie stifle a laugh, his body stiffening around her. "What did I do? You were crying when I came in. I didn't do anything!"

A lightness entered her chest, realization settling in. Kai would never do anything to hurt her. She could do this, talk to him and everything would be all right. It had to be, because Connie knew she couldn't give him up, no matter what.

"I know." The contentment in her heart let her continue. "It wasn't you. It was what I was thinking." Connie turned and straddled Kai, his constant erection settling against the softest part of her as her sundress slid up. "We need to talk."

"You keep saying that." Connie shivered, Kai shifted pressing harder against her femininity, already wet and ready for him. "So talk. Then action."

His thrust caused her whimpering, the thin barrier of her panties becoming drenched with desire. It was so hard to think when she wanted to feel the hardness of him entering her, to assuage the ache beating through her core.

"I want to be a veterinarian," Connie gasped, trying to concentrate on her words while her body burned up. "I still have a couple of years of school to go."

"I know. What's the problem?" His grunting turned her on. Kai as excited as she. His firm hands held her hips down bruising in their intensity. The shift of denim against the silkiness of her panties creating friction against her sopping wet panties. Her body shuddered. Her breath hitched, sparks flying. She gasped, shattering against him. A muffled curse and she laughed breathlessly. Connie felt Kai jerk and a warm wetness spread across her belly as she leaned against him.

"Damn it." The low curse made her giggle. "It's not funny. I haven't done that in years, decades even."

"I thought it was sexy." The vibration in his chest sounded like a growl. Connie leaned back and laughed.

"Really." She placed her mouth against his ear and licked the rim. Salt and sweat, the taste of Kai sent heat back into her groin. She shivered, her nipples tightening in anticipation.

"What did you want to talk about?" Kai settled her so she was on his lap, his arms holding her away so she could no longer lay against him. "You keep saying you want to talk, so tell me." He held her still, despite her wriggling to get closer. "We won't talk if I don't keep you at arm's length." He grinned and Connie felt her stomach jolt. It was almost feral and sent waves of heat down her back.

"I am going to school to be a veterinarian."

"So you said." He cocked his head in question. "Why is that a problem?"

"Because I can't stay here. As soon as the trial goes through and I testify, I'll be heading back to school in the fall." She looked at him, willing him to understand. "I was accepted into UW, but I still have to live there. I can't spend two hours a day driving back and forth."

"Can you spend an hour? A half hour there and back?"

"Yes, but it takes longer than that."

"You could fly."

Connie laughed at him.

"I don't have a plane or a helicopter. How could I fly?"

Kai snorted, and Connie swore it was a mix of derision and laughter.

"No, but you have a dragon."

****

Connie's look of shock sent him chuckling. Cute with nothing to say. She eyed him up before answering, obviously not sure what he meant.

"Can you explain that?"

He didn't want to. He wanted to rip off the soaking wet panties from Connie, plunge inside. Make her scream. He didn't want to talk.

His nostrils flared, the air scented with her arousal. His pants damp and sticky. He couldn't believe he'd blown his wad in his jeans like a randy teenager. Connie did things to him he never thought possible.

He wouldn't give it up for the world.

Kai listened to her concerns. He could tell that becoming a vet was important to her. He needed to keep his mate happy and safe. He ignored the heat Connie sent through his body in order to answer her.

"My home, our home is only a few minutes from here. I can fly you to school or you could fly yourself once we mated. UW is a medical facility as well as a veterinarian facility. Both their buildings have helicopter pads. Most shifters that can fly go for treatment there."

Connie's jaw slid open in surprise.

He closed it with a tip of his finger. He chuckled. "UW has been combining veterinary studies with physician studies for years. The premier shifter physicians all come from UW Madison. They learn to treat both parts of a shifter." Kai leaned in and gave Connie a soft kiss. He craved the feel of her silky lips, dipping inside her mouth, teasing her. "I'd be proud to help you achieve your goal no matter how long it takes."

Kai watched Connie. Her eyes grew bright and a blazing smile broke across her face.

"Do you mean it? You don't mind?"

Kai shook his head. "Of course I don't mind. Why would you think that would bother me?"

"I thought I'd have to stay in Madison and only see you on the weekend."

Kai chuckled, peace flowing throughout his body. She was his. It was only a matter of time before they mated. He could feel their emotional bonds entwining further. Soon only the physical claiming would be left.

"What makes you think I wouldn't stay with you in Madison?" Kai knew she didn't understand their bond. She would.

"Your job is here. Your life is here, despite the ick factor of you being friends with my grandpa."

"You are my life. I don't need this job. I've lived centuries and dragons amass treasure. I can go anywhere and do anything I please. I'm a dragon." Kai knew he sounded arrogant. Nothing he said untrue. Dragons could and did anything they pleased. "Now, what do you mean ick factor?"

Connie's eyes crinkled and sparkled before the laugh came. Kai could see it as it happened and he could feel it spreading warmth to his heart.

"Ick factor, like if you're friends with my grandpa, you've got to be old. Older than dirt. Not that you look like it, but still. Ick." Her teasing laughter made his dragon grumble.

He didn't want his mate to think of him as old. He wasn't.

"I'll show you old." Kai grabbed Connie, twisting and pinning her beneath him. Her dress wrapped around her waist, leaving her, Kai peeked, lacy yellow panties exposed. He took a claw and sliced them off her, leaving her glistening pussy exposed. Holding her down with one arm, he slid lower. His claws now fingers once again, tracing the soft petals of her engorged sex. Plump, red and swollen just for him.

Kai placed a tender kiss on her clitoris, peeking boldly from its hiding place. Connie moaned and shivered against him. Her hands slid in his hair, her hips following his lips. Kai leaned back, smirking.

"Kai, please."

"Are we done talking?"

"What?"

"Are we done talking? I don't mind you finishing

school and nothing will keep me away from my mate, from you. Is that it? Are we done?"

"Yes." Her moan sent a thrill of possession through him.

"Good. I'm hungry."

Connie gasped as he flicked his tongue on her sensitive spot. Her fingers tightening in his hair as she tried to direct him where she wanted. Kai had other ideas. He'd get where she wanted, just at his pace.

He leaned in delicately licking her, spreading her sex and lightly licking the edge of her passage. She rewarded him with her sweet cream. He moved closer, nuzzling her clit with his nose, his tongue diving in to gather every bit of her desire. Pulling back he drove his tongue into her, fucking her as her hips arched, her body eager for him. Before she could cry out, Kai moved, lips sucking in her clit, finger filling her.

He humped the edge of the bed. The heat of her slick passage pulling in his thrusting finger as he sucked her clit. In and out, harder and faster. With a wail, Connie came, her pussy clamping down as he worried her clit with his tongue, watching her fall to bits.

Unable to wait, with a last suck of her tender bits, Kai shoved his pants open and pulling her body to the edge, slammed into Connie, sliding to the hilt. She screamed again, convulsing on him. Tilting her hips toward him, surrounded by her luscious heat, Kai took Connie in a frenzy, not stopping until another orgasm shook her. Her legs wrapped around his waist, pulling him to her. Her scalding passage tightening almost painfully on him.

"Mate me?" He pushed the words out his hoarse vocal cords. She needed to accept him. He could not imagine any other outcome. He'd fuck her senseless to get her to say yes.

"Yes."

Thank God. Kai felt his incisors grow at her acceptance and he bit down, marking her breast, feeling her nipple harden as he suckled, marking her as his. Connie screamed as her body bowed once again. He exploded inside her, his cum filling her as the changes from his bite began to spread throughout her body.

Kai's dragon hummed in happiness. Connie was his.

CHAPTER SEVENTEEN

Connie woke, a strange tingling in her body. She rolled over and looked at her clock and swore. "Shit, I forgot to set the alarm."

Forgetting about the strange feelings, she jumped up and ran into the shower. Connie didn't want to be late to work during the first week. Idly, she wondered where Kai went, but considering the time, figured he was already up and working. Life didn't stop on a farm just because you wanted to sleep in. She knew that much. Connie squealed. The cold spray hit her. Quickly adjusting it to a much hotter stream, Connie lathered up. In and out in five, or close to it. She used to race her brother Mason, who always declared her the loser. A Navy man, he'd always give her grief. She grinned, rinsed, and jumped out. She would have won today.

After toweling her hair she brushed it back in a quick pony tail. Connie eyed herself in the mirror. Kai's bite mark was already healed, leaving scars behind that looked suspiciously like his scales. Just thinking about it, Connie felt a flush run up her body. She didn't have time to indulge in any hanky-panky, though, so luckily Kai wasn't in the room.

She might not be able to resist him, but he couldn't resist her either. Grinning at her reflection, she went in the bedroom and pulled out her scrubs. Dressing quickly, Connie grabbed her purse and ran into the kitchen.

"Connie, great, you're ready." Ellen slung her purse over her. "I got called into work, so I can drop you off. Breccan is going to follow us." She waved a hand at the counter. "There's a coffee mug for you and a bagel." Ellen grabbed one of the two mugs and a bagel. "Let's go."

Connie grabbed the other mug and bagel and followed her.

"Where's Breccan?"

"He's out in the truck already waiting for us. I was getting ready to wake you when I heard the shower go on."

"Thanks. I can't believe I over slept."

Ellen laughed and looked at her.

"I can." She elbowed Connie. "Bow chica wow wow."

"Oh, my God, what are you? Ten?" Connie sputtered. "Like you have any room to talk. I can hear you clear across the house."

Ellen smiled smugly. "I wouldn't change a thing." Ellen laughed and jumped in the car. Maxwell closed the door, frowning down at her.

"Be careful."

"I will."

"Let's get going, Ellen." Connie pulled on the door but it didn't shut. She looked over to see Kai leaning in, with a grin on his face.

"Don't I get a kiss goodbye?"

"Of course." Connie leaned up and slid her arms around his neck.

Kai grabbed her and pulled her toward him, half lifting her out of her seat. Connie felt everything else slipping away. Kai's warm tongue made her lips tingle before he slipped it inside, teasing her mouth. His soft lips caressed her before he pulled back, tucking her in the truck.

"Mmm. Good morning." He tasted like coffee. She loved coffee.

"Good morning." He grinned, closing the door.

"Okay, we need to get going." Ellen pressed her foot on the gas, revving up the car.

"Okay, okay." Kai stepped back and shut the door. "Connie, I'll be there to pick you up after work."

"I can pick her up. I'll already be in town." Ellen revved the engine. "We've got to get going."

"No, we're not leaving you two to come home by yourselves. Ellen you call me when you're almost done. I'll meet you and follow you to pick up Connie." Maxwell ruffled Ellen's hair. "Kai will come with and drive Connie home. We don't plan on taking any chances with you two."

"Fine. We have to go or we'll both be late." Ellen

pushed the pedal down, the car revving but held back by her foot on the brake.

Maxwell and Kai stepped back. The car shot forward. Connie watched the men get smaller in the mirror. She turned and blew a kiss to Kai, who stood watching them leave. Breccan followed in another truck, spitting up gravel so the other two ducked. Connie could see the grin on his face and his head go back in laughter as Maxwell tossed a rock after him. Kai laughed, shook his head and turned toward the barn.

"Ellen, I'm sorry for the trouble I've brought."

"Don't worry about it. If our men can't keep us safe, no one can."

"I never imagined they would really follow me here."

"We don't know for sure if they did. It could be they haven't found you."

"I don't know. I keep getting the feeling I'm being watched." Connie groaned. "And not in a good way."

Ellen snickered. "Are you sure it isn't just Kai?"

"No." Connie's cheeks warmed at the thought. "I love the way Kai watches me."

"Sick woman. Remember he's a friend of grandpa's."

"Stop! I know okay? I mentioned the ick factor to him last night and he was NOT happy."

Ellen giggled and she couldn't help but join in.

"He decided to prove he wasn't too old." Connie snorted. "He did."

****

Kai looked at his watch. He wanted to make sure they left in time to pick up Connie and Ellen. He had time to scout out the area. He swore they were being watched and it worried him. His gut was burning and he knew better than to ignore it. He shut down the computer. The farm input could wait.

"Breccan, I'm going to scout the area."

"Why? What's the matter?"

"I can't get over the feeling we're being watched. I want to check the perimeter to see if I can spot anything out of place."

"I thought maybe it was just me. Nothing moved

last night that I could see while on watch. It seemed peaceful then."

"I felt it when I was on, but it went away." Kai frowned. Knowing Breccan felt the same worried him.

"Maybe it's only when Ellen and Connie are here." Maxwell stepped in as he spoke, wiping his hands on a rag.

"I'll check around the buildings, if you two will check the edge of the farm." Breccan frowned, heading out.

Work forgotten, the safety of their mates on their minds, they split to check out the area.

Kai shifted, heading across the fields. *I'll check outside the edge of the farm if you check inside, Max. They might not be watching from Ellen's property, but from outside it.*

Sounds good.

Kai was glad dragons shared the ability to talk to any shifter species. It used to be used to lull prey into believing they were talking to one of their own. Now, it came in handy with his association with the wolves. Not that he liked touching their minds. Far from it. If he wasn't worried about Connie, he'd refrain.

Glad they had a plan and were executing it, Kai looked around with all his senses sharpened. He'd start searching the areas with a view of the house. He hoped he wouldn't find anything. He flew, heading to the back of the property. There were plenty of hillocks and stands of trees where someone could hide out, but they'd have to hike in. He saw no evidence of vehicles through the fields. The crops would have been torn up. He hovered over each of the areas. Only one showed any activity so far. From the scent, he knew it was the neighbors. They'd probably used it for a lunch break when checking on their fields. They were no threat.

Continuing toward the road, the most likely spot with a thick stand of woods across from the farm, Kai flew close to the ground. He didn't want to miss anything. He shifted, landing to get a better look. The woods thick enough that searching on two feet became easier. The trees and bushes grew too close together for his dragon. He didn't want to miss anything by accidentally stomping on it.

Kai's nose twitched. Someone passed here.

Whether it someone hiking or not, he wasn't sure yet. He turned to check out the farm. If it was someone watching them, they would want a good view of the house. Kai walked until he found the view he was looking for. Turning into the woods, he started to search.

Son of a bitch! Kai heard Breccan loud and clear.

What's the matter? Maxwell asked before he could.

We are definitely being watched. When you two finish, come to the house. I'm going to review the security tapes.

Kai never heard Breccan so fierce before. The more laid back of the two or so he thought. Breccan was definitely the alpha of the pair, but Kai wondered if that was by Maxwell's choice. He no longer wondered. The power emanating from Breccan dispelled that idea.

Kai returned to what he was doing. If Breccan found evidence at the house Kai would see if what he found was the faint scent trail he picked up.

Kai stopped, sniffing. A man's scent permeated the area. Closely checking he found a blind built to give a perfect view of the house. He swore. They were being watched. He frowned, furious. Connie wasn't going anywhere by herself until this was done. Nothing could happen to her.

I found a spot that gives a perfect view of the house. I'm going to follow it and see where it leads me.

I found nothing on the property. The drive has too many scents to pick out one. Want help following it? Maxwell sounded eager to join in, his words coming in a fierce growl. Wolves were territorial and they considered Ellen and the babies' part of their pack. Connie too, by default.

No. It appears to only be one man. So far. Smoke curled from his nostrils. He would find him and eliminate the threat to his mate.

Let me know if you need help.

Kai broke off communication. He needed to eliminate the threat. He searched the blind. The man spent several hours here, quite possibly days. Kai felt the feeling of being watched for at least that long. He should have paid attention. Grunting, he turned, following the faint trail the man left.

Kai's gut clenched. The man was a professional.

Without being able to follow his scent he wouldn't have even found a trail. Kai swore. The trail disappeared. Only the faint trace of exhaust on burned grass gave away evidence a car parked there.

Kai checked around the area, but the scent ended where the car sat. He wouldn't forget it, though. He shifted, flying from the clearing and over the trees, hoping to see if he could see anything or anyone that would direct him which way to go.

Nothing. He ground his teeth. His belly burned, wanting to light the woods on fire to eliminate the threat. Without the woods to hide in, his dragon insisted Connie would be safe. Fighting his instincts Kai turned, heading back to the farm. All he did was prove someone was watching. His gut told him that. He wondered what Breccan found to piss him off so much. Kai's gut told him he wouldn't like it any more than Breccan.

Flying in, he heard Breccan swearing and Maxwell's angry mumbling. He landed, shifted, and headed toward them.

"What did you find?"

"You're not going to like it." Breccan's words

were barely understandable. He was partially shifted, eyes gleaming yellow and deadly.

"Somehow, that doesn't surprise me." Kai strode closer and froze. His vision shifted and rumbles erupted from his chest. "I'll kill this man." Definitely a dead man walking.

"Not if we get him first." Breccan's words were flat, deadlier than Kai thought the wolf could possibly be.

Maxwell growled in agreement. "He was outside Connie's bedroom, also."

Kai's lips tightened, his nostril's flaring. A rumble and flame shot out, eliminating the evidence. His dragon rumbled in satisfaction while he acknowledged the scent was the same one from the spot in the woods.

"Holy shit!" Maxwell chuckled.

"You'll burn the house down!" Breccan turned and ran to the closest shed returning with a shovel. He quickly turned the earth and threw dirt on it, smothering it. "Damn it, Kai! What were you thinking?"

"I wasn't." He ran a hand through his hair, yanking on the ends. "I just wanted to burn the man that did this." The painful pulls relieved a bit of the churning in his guts. "If I find him first, he'll be charbroiled."

Breccan and Maxwell laughed viciously.

"You do that, old man. Just make sure we're there to help." Breccan smirked.

He gave an annoyed look at the younger wolves. Kai wasn't amused by the age reference, especially in light of Connie voicing what she called the ick factor. It wasn't age, it was experience, damn it. He'd proved that to her last night. If he needed to, he'd kick the wolves' asses from here to tomorrow, but he hunted other prey. The wolves could wait.

CHAPTER EIGHTEEN

Connie looked down at her phone. It vibrated in her pocket. *Let's go to the coffee shop when you're done. I'm on my way.* The text from Ellen sent a smile to her face. She couldn't wait to see Kai. She was surprised they would be willing to stop, but if Ellen pulled out the pregger's card the wolves would give in. Connie didn't doubt that. Idly touching her belly, Connie wondered if Kai would be better or worse than Breccan. She snorted. Worse, definitely worse. Why was she even thinking about that? She couldn't afford a pregnancy if she wanted to finish her degree.

"Hey, Lou, will coffee hurt a shifter pregnancy?"

Aidan popped his head out of the exam room he was in and sniffed.

"You're not pregnant. Yet." He grinned, a twinkle in his eye. "Don't worry about it."

"Jeesh." Connie rolled her eyes. "Not me! Ellen's pregnant and she wants to go to the coffee shop. She's pregnant with a litter." Connie snickered.

"It should be okay. Not much hurts a shifter pregnancy. Wolf, right?"

Connie nodded.

"Contrary to popular theories, not even silver can hurt a wolf." Aidan laughed. "How and why it got around a precious metal can hurt any shifter when we're so tied to the earth is ridiculous."

All day long Aidan and Lou teased her. They couldn't see her mark, but evidently being marked changed her scent. They were dropping what they called 'helpful hints' all day long. Whether or not they were true was another story. This was actually the most interesting one.

"You mean you can't kill a werewolf with silver bullets?"

Lou howled in laughter while Aidan snickered.

"No, but wolves get a kick out of selling them. They make an obscene amount doing it, too. 'Guaranteed to protect the home from werewolves or your money back.' Luckily, there are laws about not hunting werewolves or they'd lose their profit when the truth came out."

Connie felt a smile grow. She shook her head in amusement. "Don't you think it's wrong to sell something to people they know won't work?"

"Bullets will still stop them if you shoot them in the head or heart. Doesn't matter if it's silver or not. Despite everything people believe, we're not immortal. Got to finish this exam." Aidan grinned, shutting the door, and disappearing from sight.

"I don't see a mating mark." Lou slid her a sly glance. "Where did your dragon mark you?"

A flush of heat covered her body and Connie shook her head.

"None of your business."

Lou laughed as he continued entering the information from the chart in front of him.

"Has to be in a pretty good spot then to turn you into a tomato."

"Shut up." Connie couldn't help but laugh. There was no use getting mad. Lou would just tease her more. He smirked, then turned to her.

"Have you changed yet?"

"Changed? Why would I need to change? What's wrong with my scrubs?" Connie frowned twisting her head to see any spots or stains she didn't know about.

"Changed into a dragon." Lou shook his head. "Don't you know anything?"

"What are you talking about?" Kai mentioned nothing about changing. Ellen was mated for a couple of months and she never mentioned it either. Connie couldn't imagine Ellen not telling her and she definitely couldn't imagine Ellen not showing her. They would both think it the coolest thing. "I won't be able to change into a dragon, will I?"

"Of course you will." Lou frowned at her. "Didn't

the doc's brother mention anything about you changing?"

"No, just that we were mates." Connie looked down, feeling the flush rise once again. The heat of her cheeks made her want to hide. "We haven't really talked about it." At Lou's chuckle her cheeks burned even more.

"Well then, since you won't be rolling between the sheets with me." Lou winked at her, "I'll give you the need to know."

"I can do that. I'm a dragon, after all. Not to mention a doctor." Aidan was escorting his patient out. "Lou can check you out." He handed the folder to Lou.

The old man looked back at the room they left. "Are you sure he has to stay?" His voice quavered.

"Yes. Spot will be ready to pick up tomorrow. I'll have him ready to go." Aiden placed a hand on his shoulder.

"Okay. He might get lonely without me."

"I'll leave the radio on for him. He'll be sleeping most of the night."

The man sighed. "Okay, Doc, I'll pick him up tomorrow."

"Sure, boss. You go right ahead." Lou opened the

folder, his fingers flying across the keyboard. "You're the expert. You're right." Lou turned to the patient's caretaker. "Mr. Leary, Spot will be fine. Do you want to pay up today or tomorrow when you're back?"

"Tomorrow, if that's okay."

"Great. We'll see you in the morning. Good night, Mr. Leary."

They all watched the old man leave. Connie thought he would be the one lonely tonight. It was evident from his lagging steps.

"I don't know why I keep you on." Aidan grumbled at Lou, picking the conversation back up.

"I'm worth my weight in gold. You'd be lost without me. You don't pay me enough."

"Well, get over the idea you're worth your weight in gold. A dragon would never give up gold."

"Will someone tell me what changes I can expect?" Connie decided if she didn't interrupt she wouldn't find out what she wanted to know.

"I gather my brother hasn't said anything." Aidan lifted an eyebrow. It was a sexy look, but left Connie unaffected. Aidan couldn't hold a candle next to Kai, at least in her opinion. "You'll be able to talk telepathically, you'll age slower, and you can change into a dragon."

"I'll be able to talk with anyone?"

"No, just other shifters, once you get the hang of it. Primarily your mate, but you can speak to others if you try. You just have to practice."

"Right." Connie raised a brow at him. "I'll also be able to change into a dragon."

"Of course."

"Riiiight." Connie sighed. "When will I supposedly be able to do that?"

Aidan frowned.

"You should be able to now, I'd imagine." He tapped his chin. "No, now that I think about it, I seem to recall that a mate will change only after the mating bite and a full moon."

"That's insane."

Aidan looked at her and burst out laughing.

"You got me." He smiled at her. "But you should have seen your face. There is something other than the bite, but you don't look like you've been washed in dragon fire yet."

Connie thought of the heat that radiated through her last night. She wondered if that was the dragon fire. Hot as it was, she thought maybe so. She couldn't imagine anything hotter. She couldn't be sure though.

"Well, I can't change. I don't know how. Ellen has yet to change and she's been mated for a couple of months already." Connie shook her head. "I wish you two would quit pulling my leg."

"Why on earth won't you believe me?" Aidan sounded a bit baffled.

"You're telling the truth? I'll really be able to change into a dragon? How come Ellen hasn't changed? She's been mated for months."

"She really hasn't changed yet?" Lou looked interested in that news.

"What kind of shifter is her mate? Wolf, right?" Aiden quirked a brow her way.

"Yes, Breccan's a wolf."

"What kind?" Lou was the biggest busy body Connie met.

"There are more than one kind?" Connie thought a wolf was a wolf.

"Oh yes, more than you can imagine. Just as humans have different nationalities, there are different species within species."

"Huh, and Ellen will be able to change into one." Connie leaned against the counter. "And I'll be able to become a dragon. You're not just teasing me."

"No. You'll really be able to change." Aiden sounded serious. How crazy was that?

"How on earth will I do that?" Maybe she should find out more. She and Kai hadn't done a whole lot of talking together.

"Your mate will take you through it. Ellen's mate should have taken her through hers by now."

"Breccan can't have. She'd have shown me."

"Hmm. Sometimes a new shifter will only change in times of emotional upset or stress. A new mate can go years without changing. Especially since she got pregnant so fast."

"So, it's possible then that Ellen hasn't changed yet. She's been too happy to stress out." Connie smiled, thinking of how happy her cousin was. She worried her bottom lip.

Aidan nodded while Lou listened eagerly. Connie thought shifters must guard their secrets well. Lou looked like it was all new information for him, too. The pain in her lip stopped her and brought her attention back to what she heard.

"It's possible. Wolves are a bit volatile, so it's a bit surprising. A fire dragon, though, and Kai and I are fire dragons, have to be with their mates through the first change."

"Huh." Connie wondered when Kai planned on telling her. He left and returned later to her bed, then disappeared again when she got up.

"Ask Kai. Have him take you out to the fields and change. Then have him show you his lair."

"His lair?"

"Every dragon has a lair. It's where we keep our treasure. I assure you, Kai has a lair."

Connie frowned. It sounded surreal. She wondered if Aidan was messing with her again, but he looked serious. She had questions, but decided most of them could be answered by Kai.

"So, Ellen should be able to change? It won't hurt

her or the babies if she changes?"

"Nope, it won't. I'm surprised she hasn't changed yet. Babies?" Aidan cocked a brow at her.

"Yes, Ellen's carrying triplets. I'm sure I told you."

"Huh. It used to be common for a dragon to have multiples, but not so much anymore. Wolves, however, do tend to have litters. Well, she should come in for an exam."

"She's already been to the doctor."

"Probably not a shifter doctor. The Ob Gyn in town is good, but sometimes, especially with a multiple pregnancy, a shifter doctor is needed."

"I really don't want to ask, but why?"

"The babies can get a little rowdy in the delivery room." Aidan grinned at her and before she could ask any more questions, walked away. "I have to get Mr. Leary's Spot settled."

She turned to Lou, who poorly hid his interest in the conversation.

"What do you know? Why hasn't Ellen changed? Do you think anything is wrong with her?"

"Well, I'm no expert, but I doubt anything is wrong. Her mate would have called. He just may not have shown her how to change or she just hasn't told you about it."

"She would have told me. I don't think she knows she'll change. There's no way she would have kept it to herself." Connie pushed off of the counter she'd been resting on, heading back to finish cleaning up the stockroom. "There's no way we can shift. They're just pulling my leg," Connie muttered to herself, shaking her head at the thought.

"I'll let you know when your ride's here," Lou hollered.

Connie waved in acknowledgement. She entered the stockroom to replenish the supplies she'd used.

****

Breccan's phone rang, interrupting their work. Maxwell and Kai watched as Breccan answered.

"I'm done with work. I'm heading over to the vets to wait for Connie." Kai swore at the conversation he heard between Breccan and Ellen.

"I told you to call me when you were almost done." Breccan's tone was hard.

"I forgot."

"Wait for us at work. I don't want you going to pick up Connie by yourself." Breccan's aggravation was loud and clear to Kai, but evidently not to Ellen, based on her next words.

"It'll be fine. I'll see you there. I have enough time to get a coffee next door."

"Wait for us," Breccan growled as he spoke.

Kai looked at him, surprised to see him so aggravated at Ellen. He was obviously more worried than he let on about the situation, Kai realized. He could only hope Connie was taking it seriously. He stifled his doubts though.

Ellen on the other hand was finally feeling safe and he hoped this situation with Connie didn't set her back. Kai never again wanted to see the look on her face when she came back home. Aggravating as the wolves could sometimes be, they loved Ellen unconditionally and took her safety seriously. Both her mate and his beta would give their lives to protect her. A few months ago she wouldn't even have considered going somewhere by herself. Their protection and care helped Ellen regain her confidence. The timing just sucked.

"Don't worry. I'll meet you there. Love you." The easy teasing tone of her voice did nothing to reassure her mate as she hung up.

Breccan's rumble reflected his frustration.

Kai's curse echoed Maxwell's.

"Damn it." Maxwell turned to Kai. "You heard her. Let's go."

Kai was already ahead of him. He'd grabbed the keys to the truck and was heading out the door. The proof they'd found earlier, that they were being watched forefront in his mind. They hadn't time to tell the girls about the unwelcome and disturbing discovery at the house. Connie and Ellen had no idea how serious this really was. Kai knew they thought they were being overly cautious. If anything, Kai thought they all underestimated the danger.

Maxwell and Breccan swung into the cab.

Kai gunned the truck, pulling out, stones spinning

from beneath the wheels.

"We don't know they are in danger." Maxwell tried the voice of reason, but the worry in his tone made it sound more like a question.

"I'd rather not take a chance." Breccan's strained voice whispered through the cab.

Kai ignored their words. His worry increased as he drove. Something was not right. He could feel the danger in the air. The evidence of how close the unknown man was to the house, the unmitigated gall made his hackles rise. Kai's blood rose hotly, only the need for all of them to arrive in one piece keeping him from changing in the truck. The thrum of the blood pounding in his temple, his grip on the steering wheel, and the changing of his sight as he drove forced him to acknowledge his dragon was close to the edge, too close. Kai took a deep breath, forcing his dragon back.

"We'll get there and they will be fine. You'll see." Maxwell tried to sound up beat. He didn't succeed.

Breccan's growl was Maxwell's only answer. Kai assumed they were picking up on his tension. Ellen hadn't a care in the world, at least as far as Kai could tell by her voice when she hung up on Breccan. Kai hoped he was wrong. He hoped the feeling of dread growing in him was an overreaction. No one in town would dare cross him. His scent told other shifters Connie was his. The problem, the men after Connie wouldn't have any idea they were shifters.

Aiden.

I'm busy.

Keep Connie at work until I'm there. Ellen too.

I'll let her know as soon as I finish.

It can't wait.

Fine.

Kai hoped Aiden kept both women at the clinic. Kai knew no one in town would talk about them to strangers. If they managed to get Connie and Ellen alone, Kai didn't know what the stalker would do. Ellen was a wolf but hadn't changed yet. Connie couldn't change until he washed her in dragon fire. Kai even mentioned it to her. He clenched his hands. One way or another, it could only lead to disaster.

"We're almost there."

Kai glanced over and he could see Breccan and

Maxwell holding hands, their knuckles white with tension. Wolves always needed the touch of their pack for comfort. Theirs was a pack of three, soon to be six. His hands tightened reflexively on the wheel until he heard a crack. "Fuck."

They were close to town. The vet's just a little further away.

"There. I see Ellen's truck. It's just pulling in." Breccan sounded relieved.

Kai let out a breath. There in front of them was proof their mates were okay. Ellen stepped out of the truck and stuck her head in the door of the vets. They were too far away to hear her, but they saw her wave and she stepped back, shut the door and headed to the coffee shop. Kai saw Connie come out, look around frowning and then head toward the shop behind Ellen. Damn it, Aiden must not have told them to stay. Or more likely, they didn't listen.

They were safe. Three sighs were let out. Kai let up on the gas. They would be there soon enough.

"I'm going to talk to my brother, real quick, while the girls are in the shop." Kai turned in, parking next to

Ellen's vehicle.

"I'll come in, too. I want to check with Doc to see if he thinks we need an appointment for Ellen." Breccan looked worried all over again. Knowing his mate was expecting triplets he fluctuated between pride and worry. Aiden would know what to say to him.

Kai took a quick look around, peeking in the window of the coffee shop. Seeing Connie and Ellen sitting at a table in an almost empty room, he motioned to the wolves.

"They should be fine for a bit." Maxwell sounded almost as if he was asking.

Breccan nodded in agreement. "They don't look like they planned on leaving anytime soon."

Kai nodded, his chest loosening. Connie should be safe for a few minutes. He could see Ellen's car and they would have to pass by the window before they could leave. It should be safe enough. They were in public view.

CHAPTER NINETEEN

"Ellen, where's Kai?" Connie hurried after Ellen letting the door shut with a bang. She hoped she didn't damage it, rushing to follow her cousin. She'd been anticipating Kai. Behind her, Aiden called her name. Ellen's answer pulled her attention away.

"I assume at the farm."

"What do you mean? I thought we were being picked up?"

"We're fine. They are just being a group of worry warts. I'm tired of being afraid, Connie."

"We really do have something to be afraid of now,

Ellen. You can't just ditch them."

Ellen spun around, flinging her arms in the air, walking and talking backwards.

"Connie, look around. No one is after us, the guys are at home. I'm so happy to be able to walk into a store and not be afraid."

"Ellen…"

"Connie…" Ellen mocked back. "Come on, we're safe. Right here next to Kai's brother. And I'd bet the guys are on their way here now." She laughed. "Call and see if I'm not right."

Connie shook her head, pursing her lips, trying not to smile. The guys were almost unbearable. Plus, Ellen looked so happy. Connie couldn't refuse her.

"Usually I'm the one pushing the limits. I'm not used to you doing it anymore." Connie smiled at Ellen. "I'm glad you're back." She hugged Ellen.

"I'm feeling like my old self again. I'm happy. I'm loved. Life couldn't get any better."

The two laughed, linked arms and headed into the coffee shop.

They stopped at the counter, looking over the

menu items and perusing the display cabinet of sweets. Connie's neck prickled. She glanced back and noticed a man sitting at a table staring at them. Connie tried to ignore him, but kept looking back. Something about the man made her uneasy.

"What can I get for you, young ladies?" Margaret was behind the counter, smiling at them. Connie felt more at ease. Another face from her childhood, Meg, their babysitter once upon a time.

"I'll have a blueberry scone, the peppermint brownie and a large s'mores frappe." Ellen practically drooled looking into the pastry case.

"Are you sure that's enough?" Connie couldn't help teasing her. "There are still more choices left."

"Just wait until you're pregger's! We'll see how you laugh then." Ellen smiled at Meg. "Ignore her."

"Whatever. Meg, I'll have a peppermint brownie and a large grasshopper frappe."

"Ellen, are you pregnant?" Connie could hear the excitement in Meg's voice. "When did you find out? And when are you due?" Meg leaned over the counter to look at her tummy. "You've a while yet. You're not even showing."

Ellen laughed and patted her belly.

"I just found out. We haven't figured out the due date yet, but I'd guess sometime in February."

"Congratulations, Ellen. I'm so happy for you!" Meg was all smiles. "Now, let me get you your orders."

Ellen sat down at a stool along the counter. Connie turned and leaned back against the counter. She could see the man out of the corner of her eye. He was reading the paper, but Connie watched him lower it and look over at them again. He saw Connie looking at him and he snapped the paper pulling it higher, obscuring her view. She turned to Ellen and grinned.

"You know, it will be all over town tonight. Meg won't be able to keep the news to herself."

"I think she already started." Ellen laughed and pointed. Connie turned and couldn't help but join in. Meg was fixing their iced coffees while chattering over the phone stuck to her ear. "I think they'll all know before supper."

Connie felt the laughter bubble out and released it. It made her realize she'd been under more tension than she thought. Ellen was right. They didn't have anything to fear. It was daytime and they were in a public place. Her stomach tingled. Not to mention, she'd bet Kai would be here soon.

"This was a good idea Ellen. Why don't we just enjoy this here? I'll call Kai and see where they are at."

Connie dialed and Kai's phone went to voice mail. She pursed her lips, blowing a raspberry. "He forgot to charge it or he can't hear it or he turned it off. Any way I look at it, I can't reach him."

"Girls, your drinks are ready."

Connie stood up, waving Ellen back down as she started to stand. "I'll get them."

She headed to the counter and paid for the drinks and desserts. Carrying them back to the table, Connie noticed the man once again watching them. Sitting down, she glanced back at him then turned to Ellen.

"Ellen, do you know that guy over there?"

Ellen turned and looked at him, staring until he turned away.

"No. Do you?"

"Why would I ask if you knew him if I did?"

Connie's pulse beat a little faster. She took a drink, swallowed and began sucking in warm air. The air in the coffee shop did little to relieve the sharp pain in her temple.

Ellen shrugged and took a bite of brownie.

Connie squeezed the bridge of her nose, rubbed her temple and glanced at the man in question from under her lashes. She watched the man look down and then pull out his phone. Connie looked away as he dialed and began a conversation too low for her to hear.

"He's been staring at us since we came in."

"Maybe he thinks we're hot." Ellen's reply was garbled, the brownie disappearing from sight. "Oh God, that was good. I think I'll get another one before we leave."

Connie laughed and shook her head, just because Kai was paranoid didn't mean she needed to be. She watched Ellen eyeing up the bakery counter, dismissing the man from her thoughts. "You still have your scone to eat."

"Taste yours, you'll understand."

Connie leaned back, sipping her frappe. She bit

into the brownie and moaned. "Holy cow, that's good." Connie licked her fingers, getting every bit of chocolate in her mouth.

"Told you."

"I think we need to get a box of them. They'd be great dessert for dinner tonight."

"If they last past the drive home."

They laughed. Connie knew Ellen wasn't really joking. The chocolate melted in her mouth as she took another bite, the peppermint a cool accompaniment. Her taste buds savored the darkly decadent sweet as she chewed. It was almost, almost too much.

"Meg, box us up a dozen of the brownies, if you have enough, okay? We've got to take some home." Ellen spoke loud enough to catch Meg's attention.

Connie took another bite, moaning. Her mouth begged for more. She savored the chocolatey sweetness. It was almost better than sex. Almost.

"Sure thing, Ellen." Meg chattered on her cell as she pulled them out of the display and boxed up a dozen of the delicious treats. "It's a new recipe. I was searching online last night and came across these. I take it you like them."

"Love them, Meg. They are melt in your mouth delicious." Ellen broke off a bit of her scone, popping it into her mouth. "Mmm."

"Thanks." Meg looked thrilled at Ellen's praise. "I want to start doing a variety of brownies. It was so hot and peppermint just struck me as being a delicious piece of winter in an otherwise hot summer."

"I think they would be great anytime of the year, Meg." Ellen nodded. "But you're right, they are a blast of coolness, absolutely scrumptious."

"You're such a sweetie! I'll just give you a baker's dozen." Meg finished packing and tying up the box. "Here it is. It comes to twenty-five dollars. Just pay when you're ready to go. I'll be in the kitchen, just ring the bell if you need anything else."

Connie finished the brownie, scavenging crumbs from the parchment. If it wouldn't look too uncouth, she'd lick the paper making sure not a bit was left behind. She'd happily make herself sick eating them.

Meg set the box on the counter smiling as she turned. It lit up the room. Connie couldn't help but smile back. Meg seemed happy in her chosen career. Connie supposed doing what you loved did that. Meg always baked treats while babysitting. It made her the most popular sitter in the neighborhood. Connie watched her head into the back room humming.

Ellen polished off the scone and both of them were down to the end of their frappes. With a final pull of the straw, rattling the ice cubes and making too much noise they finished.

"I'll get the brownies. I plan on eating most of them." Ellen laughed and jumped up, fishing money out of her pocket to toss on the counter as she grabbed the box. "Money's on the counter, Meg."

"Thanks, Ellen. You girls enjoy." She waved peeking from the kitchen before ducking back in.

"No way. We split them." It might just be a friendly fight. No way was Ellen eating all of them.

"We'll see." Ellen laughed and headed to the door. She stopped. A man entered almost hitting her with the door. "Excuse me."

"I don't think so, bitch." He stood blocking the door. "These the birds, Fred?"

Connie started backing up, grabbing Ellen's arm and pulling her away. The man at the table folded the newspaper and stood. His grin was vicious.

"The blonde is the nark. The other insurance."

Connie's stomach sank, the sweetness of the brownie turning sour and sitting heavy in her stomach. They were after her.

"Ellen, run."

They turned, but were unable to get away. The men caught them as they turned to flee. They dragged them out the door, muffling their screams with an arm around each of their necks.

"Shut up, bitch, or I'll shoot you right here."

Connie felt the gun jabbed into her side. Her past just caught up with her. She only hoped Meg saw and called the police.

****

Kai looked up. He could hear police sirens coming closer. Breccan stilled and then turned, running toward the door, Maxwell on his heels.

Kai froze then ran after them, his brother and Lou on his heels behind him. Kai exited into his worst nightmare. Ellen and Connie were being dragged by two men, one with a gun.

Kai growled. One dead man held a gun against Connie's side. Her lips trembled and her chest rose and fell showing her panic. Kai smelled her fear. He should have turned her. Breccan and Maxwell were likewise at a standoff. Ellen struggled in the grasp of a second man. The sounds of sirens coming closer. The men holding the women glanced around nervously.

Kai could see the anger rising off of Ellen, suppressing the fear in her eyes. The man holding her jammed a gun against her visible stomach, just beginning to show signs of the precious load she was carrying. Ellen's eyes flashed, her scream of outrage turned to a roar and the gunman screamed as Ellen shifted for the first time, her emotions pulling out her wolf to protect her.

She turned to face her attacker. She lunged at him, catching him by the arm with her mouth and tossing him to the ground, his gun clattering away. Ellen pounced on him, his moan loud as she landed on him, making her wolf smile with obvious satisfaction. Ellen became the predator.

Ellen moved, making sure to keep her attacker pinned and with a snap of teeth and eyes shooting sparks, swung toward the man holding Connie. He jammed the gun against Connie's temple.

"Freeze bitch. I don't need her alive."

Breccan, Maxwell and Kai surged up behind him.

Lou cocked a shotgun, freezing the man in place. "Let her go."

Kai hadn't even realized Lou was armed.

"I'll shoot her." The man pressed the gun harder against her skin.

Kai wanted to rip his head from his body and crunch his bones, savoring the warm blood of his enemy. A growl tore from his throat. A fucking standoff. The bastard was dead, but not before he released Connie.

"You'll be dead too then." Lou shouldered the gun, the man in his sites.

"Fuck." He dropped his gun to the ground. Kai surged forward, wrapping Connie in his arms. Her limbs trembled against him. He couldn't pull her close enough.

Breccan and Maxwell grabbed the man by the arms. Breccan kicked the gun away.

"Doc, we need something to tie them up with."

Aidan nodded and headed into his clinic. He returned and handed Max a roll of duct tape. Max tied him up, taping him from wrist to elbow. He grabbed the man's feet and hogtied him, dropping his body carelessly to the ground and making sure he couldn't move.

Kai smiled, baring his sharp teeth. The man blanched, shrinking in on himself. Aiden clapped a hand on his shoulder.

It's not worth it. With all the witnesses he'll go to prison for a long time.

Kai growled and embraced Connie tighter. Aiden was right as much as he didn't want to admit it.

Lou stood guard over him, shotgun aimed at his belly. Breccan and Maxwell straightened up, turning toward Ellen.

"Ellen, honey, let him go now. We have him," Breccan told her, nodding at the man she was sitting on.

They moved toward Ellen. She moved off of the

man, growling, daring him to make a run for it. Max moved forward to tie up the man. Breccan knelt, wrapping his arms around Ellen.

"You're beautiful."

The men captured, Kai turned his attention back to his mate. She'd stopped trembling but buried her face in his neck. He could have lost her. Rage rose in him again. His talons erupted from his fingertips. He just found her and he'd almost lost her. He pulled her even tighter against him. He wanted blood.

"I could've lost you." Kai ran his hands up and down her body. His heart hurt at the thought. He should have made sure she was safe. He never should have left the two of them alone. "Are you hurt?"

"No." Connie buried her face in his chest, holding tight. Connie sobbed on his shoulder. "I thought we were going to die."

Meg ran out of the shop, a box in her hand, looking around wildly.

"I called the police. I saw them drag you girls out. You dropped this."

Aidan stepped to her, grabbing the box and settling

an arm over her shoulder.

"Thank you, Meg. You did good."

She beamed at him and turned toward Ellen, her jaw dropping.

"That's Ellen?" Meg sounded awed. Kai couldn't help chuckling.

"Ellen?" Connie pulled from Kai's arms, wiping her eyes as tears streamed down her face. "Ellen, are you okay?"

Ellen nudged her with her head, and snorted at her.

"Ellen. Ellen, you're a wolf! Oh my God! You're a wolf!" Connie stopped crying, looking at her in amazement. "Ellen that is so cool!" She circled Ellen. Now that the danger was controlled, she ignored the men on the ground. "Wow! Change back now. I want to see you do it again."

Ellen preened and then growled at her. Maxwell laughed as he and Breccan dragged the man from under Ellen's paw, leaving both men under Lou's watchful eye and shotgun.

"Uh, Connie, I'm thinking she doesn't know how yet." Ellen growled at Breccan. "It's all right, honey. It's easy once you've changed the first time."

The sounds of sirens rose in a shriek of ear splitting noise. Lights flashed all around, the red and blue strobes lending a surreal effect to the scene. Kai couldn't stand it, he pulled Connie back into his arms, her softness tight against him. He never wanted to let her go again.

Ellen was growling at the men, who no longer looked dangerous, only scared as they tried to get away from her, unable to do more than rock the way they were taped up.

"You're beautiful." Breccan ran a hand down her head, scratching behind Ellen's ear.

"Dangerous." Maxwell chuckled, admiration in his voice.

The whispers Breccan and Maxwell used were soothing Ellen's wolf. Kai couldn't help but chuckle. Females of all species were vain creatures and the litany of praise that Ellen received from her mate and her beta inflated her wolf up in obvious pleasure.

The officers on the scene approached carefully.

"Which one of you is Meg?"

"That's me."

"You called this in?" Meg nodded. "I'll need to get your statement in a bit." He walked over to where Lou was watching the prisoners. "I can take over from here." Lou nodded and stepped back as the officer and his partner looked down at the prisoners. "You have the right to remain silent."

Kai tuned out the reading of the Miranda Rights, his attention centered on Connie. The scent of her had him nuzzling the top of her head, breathing deep as he enjoyed the whisper of jasmine from her hair.

"Kai, did Ellen really change into a wolf? I can hardly believe it." Connie's whisper barely made it to his ears. She buried her head in his chest again.

"Look for yourself." He nudged her head around, and loosened his arms as she turned, staying in his embrace. He sighed in contentment as she leaned against his strength, snuggling into his embrace while his arms wrapped around her even tighter. Her curves settled against him, rousing him.

"That's truly Ellen?" Her voice sounded awed.

"Yes. As far as I know, today was the first time she shifted."

"That's awesome." Her voice trailed off as she watched her cousin preen under the whispers of her pack mates.

"You know, you'll be able to change once I've washed you in dragon fire."

Kai could feel her shiver as his breath wafted past her ear.

"I'm not sure what that is."

"Don't worry, you'll enjoy it." His voice went guttural thinking about it. Now that he'd injected dragon serum into her system from his bite she could withstand the mating fire. He couldn't wait to show her.

EPILOGUE

Connie shivered, tingles running up and down her body with the feel of Kai's hands. His callouses rough against her smooth skin. The heat of his skin contrasting with the cool air of the cavern they were in.

"This is your lair?"

"Yes. Do you like it?"

"It's unusual." She felt hot, her skin heating as Kai continued to touch her. It was a cave, nothing to enthuse over, not like the feel of Kai's hands. She wanted them all over her.

"I plan to expand the existing house. Would you

like that?"

"Yes!" It was cute, but small. Connie would need an office for homework and study, though a bedroom sounded great right now.

Kai pulled her after him, sending butterflies fluttering through her veins, heading deeper into the cavern and around a natural wall.

"This is the heart of my cavern."

Kai stepped back and Connie gasped. The light sparkled off of the walls, a polished crystal, veined with gold. She looked closer. "Are the walls diamond? How on earth…"

Kai chuckled. "Yes."

It was stunning. In the center, spilling to embrace the walls were Kai's treasures; Gold and precious gems mounded around the cavern covering the floor, while art work, delicate statuary, and intricate porcelains from around the world were displayed in sparkling niches around the cave.

"It's beautiful."

Connie stepped forward, the sight dazzling her. Kai's arms encircled her waist, pulling her against him, his heat warming her skin. Desire pooled low in her abdomen. His touch and the sight of the gold awakened something inside of her.

"It is yours, too."

Connie turned around to face him, throwing her arms around him. She plastered his face with kisses, then pulled back to look in his eyes.

"It's perfect." Connie cocked her head and looked at him. "We will live above ground, won't we?"

Kai chuckled and pulled her against him. Connie moaned at the feel of his hard body against hers. He began stripping her, peppering each reveal with kisses and licks.

How could she even think about a house with him touching her? Connie shivered, goose bumps racing across her body. She wanted more. She wanted all of Kai.

"Yes." He licked her neck, nibbling at the soft skin. Tremors pricked through her, tightening her nipples and causing an ache between her legs. Connie lifted her leg, tucking it around his hips and pulling him in closer.

His hard length burned hot against her aching pussy. She wanted him naked. Connie undulated on him, moisture coating his pants as she rubbed against him, moaning at the friction against her clit.

Kai groaned and stripped, talons slashing while he tore his clothes away in his eagerness. Connie watched as he stepped from his shoes and the remains of his pants, her pussy hot and wet. She ached for him.

"Kai."

Kai pulled her to him. Connie wrapped her legs around his waist, his hardness sliding in her slick heat.

Kai groaned and pulled her off of him. The achy feeling of emptiness had her reaching once again toward him. She *needed* him.

Kai laughed and tossed her onto the gold. The sudden cold and sound of coins sliding to accommodate her sending a shiver through her body. Connie relaxed on her back, stretching her arms and legs against the gold beneath her. The gold and gems sent a sensuous thrill through her. She wiggled to shift into a comfortable position or rather, tried. Kai watched her. The glitter in his eyes thrilled her. She ignored the edges of the coins digging in her back. Unimportant compared to the adoration in his eyes.

"Come to me." Connie spread out her arms needing to feel the press of Kai's body.

Kai gazed down at her, his eyes burning hotly, his dragon evident in every line of his face. He kneeled before her, spreading her legs further apart. Connie flushed, her blood heating at the look of lust on his face.

"Mine." His guttural tone had her almost cumming on the spot.

Kai drove forward, spearing her with his cock. She cried out, as he thrust endlessly into her, shudders racking her. His eyes changed, and Connie could see the dragon coming out to play. Her sheath tightened, her nipples pebbling at the fullness inside. The ripple of the veins on his penis throbbing as he thrust inside of her, sent thrills along her spine. His deliciousness sent all thoughts of the uncomfortable pile beneath her away.

Connie loved the heat of him inside her, the juices that flowed from her, easing his passage as he fucked her. Her eyes transfixed on the sight of him and her. Him in her.

"Look at me."

Connie looked up, shifting her gaze to his eyes.

"Kiss me." Kai's voice was deep, rough.

Connie leaned forward, arching. Kai pulled her up, settling her firmly on his thighs, his cock throbbing hotly in her pussy. He lifted her and pushed her down on him, settling deeper inside her.

She reached and wrapped her arms and legs around him. Connie groaned in pleasure, wiggling until there was no more space between them. She heard a coin drop, felt it peel from her skin to clatter down with the rest.

Connie giggled. Now, the only poking going on from her mate. Kai growled and moved. Connie forgot all about anything but the hard length inside of her, scalding her and sending shivers through her.

Connie wiggled. Her clit was nestled against the springy hair surrounding his penis. Her breasts flattened against his muscles. He shifted her, rubbing her breasts against him, her clit deliciously tingling. She moaned. She'd never get enough.

"Open for me." Kai leaned down and kissed her, his tongue seeking hers. His hands gripping her hips, pressing her down as he arched deeper into her. Filling her again and again as his mouth devoured her.

"Take all of me." Kai tilted forward pinching her nipples, pressing her back into the gold. Connie couldn't move, just feel and enjoy. The pain turning to pleasure as his weight pressed upon her. Her nipples hard and reaching for more of his touch. Her clit throbbing and begging as the blood rushed to the nerves centered there. Kai slid his thumb down and rubbed, his callouses flickering against her sensitive bundle and then he pinched her.

Connie convulsed, her pussy clenching and releasing on Kai's cock. His thrusts making her climb higher and higher as she flew over the edge.

Kai's lips sealed to hers. Fire poured from his mouth as he emptied himself into her with frantic pumps of his hips. She screamed. Connie's arms and legs surrounded him, pulling closer as the agonizing pleasure washed through her. Her body shuddering, her pussy clenching to keep Kai from leaving each time he slid in and out of her.

Her keening echoed around the walls as the heat enveloped her. The fire began to die and her arms and legs dropped, exhaustion over taking her. Connie could feel Kai still pulsing inside her. The delicious length and ripples of his cock caressing her pussy over and over.

"I'll never get enough of you." His voice was deep and rough. His hips swiveled against her, dragging another moan from her throat.

"So that was dragon fire." Connie shivered. "Does this mean I can become a dragon, too?" She didn't know how she managed to find the strength to speak.

"Yes. Our mating is complete." Kai grinned at her, licking her throat.

His next kiss was deep, his tongue caressing the depths of hers. His lips soft despite their firmness. His hands slid down her silken curves, caressing every inch of her body.

"I love you, Kai." Connie sighed, her voice hoarse. "But next time, a bed."

"I love you, too, my treasure." Kai chuckled, pulling her close.

THE END

• ABOUT THE AUTHOR

Beverly Ovalle dabbled with writing on and off for years when her best friend finally dared her to submit a story to a writing contest. Beverly decided she had nothing to lose and since she'd always wanted to be an author sent it in and agonized for months waiting to hear back. Contract in hand she has never looked back.

Beverly has been obsessed with dragons and romance since she was a young girl, collecting dragon books and reading everything she could find on them even down to the care of real life dragons. She's always been slightly panicked that the world as we know it will end, so has prepped for it, haunting survivalist pages and prepper projects she felt she needed in the event SHTF.

An avid fan of all romance, Beverly's goal is to share her love of the written word and write the hot and erotic romances that she enjoys. She writes what she loves to read and it was only a matter of time before her obsessions crept into her writing for her to share. She hopes you enjoy her tales as much as she loves writing them.

A Navy Veteran, Beverly has traveled around the world and the United States enabling her to bring her settings to life, meeting and marrying her husband of twenty five years along the way for her own romance. Reading romances since the fourth grade she's followed as the genre changed and spread into the vast cornucopia of romance offered today.

Find my other books at Amazon, Kobo, iTunes,

Barnes & Noble and other eRetailers.

Dragons' Mate

They had been searching for their mate, but when they find her she is traumatized and scared to be around strange men. They must get her to accept them before they reveal their true natures. Will their love be strong enough to break down her barriers? Could she truly be destined to love two dragons?

Today Annie's dragons will shift and fulfill her every desire, which means a fiery threesome—and true love.

Stealing Hope

The apocalypse has come and gone.
Those who survived learned to adapt.
Dragons awaken to once again reign over the skies.

Upon eruption of a volcano, Ari awakens to a changed world, and a knowing that his dragon's mate is near. He saves her twice—once as a dragon, and again as a man—and wins her confidence.

Hope cried out, moaning, "just change me with pleasure?"

Hope is restless and unfulfilled until she meets Ari, the man of her fantasies. The sensual tension between them heightens with every touch. When their passion explodes, Hope gets pulled into the dragon's mating ritual...and into a world of erotic sensation she never dreamed existed but now cannot live without. The dragon binds his mate to him with a ritual that shows Hope her true nature in this humorous erotic romance.

Rise of the Dragons: a Dragon's Fated Heart prequel

The apocalypse has come.

Dragons awaken to once again reign over the skies.
Dax and Jasima explore and try to save what they can of mankind.

Their children's future depends on it.

Lightning Strike

For generations Levi's family had guarded a sacred glen in the mountains. Still far from man this isolated area was a favorite spot of his grandfather. Levi grew up listening to his tales and fell in love without ever having stepped foot there.

Now Levi's family, led by his grandmother, wanted to sell the land. With only his grandfather and Levi against it, Levi has to prove to the rest of the family why they needed to continue their guardianship. Believing in his grandfather's tales despite himself, Levi went armed with his camera and his well-known expertise behind the lens and headed out for proof.

Providing that proof and protecting the secrets of the glen from the world, Gaia needs to convince Levi to continue that protection. Daphnaie, the embodiment of his every dream, is sent to show him why, stealing his heart in the process to save her world.

Touched by the Sandman

A lonely woman's torrid sexual dreams and fantasy partner await her as a dominant reality in another dimension.

The sandman visits those that need him, assisting them to sleep. Until one night he meets a woman that he cannot help but return to time after time.

She is lonely. He comes to her as she drifts off to sleep, the man of her dreams. Awake or asleep, which is her reality?

He knows she is the one meant for him. He will find a way to make both of their dreams come true.

Triple D Dude Ranch

Blaire had gotten an exciting assignment, sending her from Chicago back home to Texas. She was taking pictures of a dude ranch for the Tribune, an up and coming vacation spot for the city slicker. Blaire couldn't help the wildfire of desire that ran through her at the uninhibited cowboy she finds in the lens of her camera.

Dan remade his ranch, making it a go to vacation spot being featured in the vacation section in a Chicago newspaper. A freelance photographer was coming to take pictures for the article. Dan couldn't believe the hot and sassy urban cowgirl that arrived, camera in hand.

Texas is hot as hell. But it is nothing compared to the fire that blazes instantly between Blaire and Dan. Just one look, one touch, Blaire was the spark and Dan was the tinder that fed those flames, sparking a conflagration that nothing can stop.

Love Me Forever

Staff Sergeant Liam McGregor doesn't know what hit him. Sent home to recuperate from an IED blast, Liam is stuck in a wheelchair and is sentenced to surgery and physical therapy before he can walk again.

A physical therapist, Abby Worth has loved Liam McGregor since she first noticed boys. It's too bad he's her brother's best friend. She has always been firmly put in the baby sister zone no matter how hard she tried to catch his eye.

Liam sees Abby and when she goes home with him doesn't know how he can keep his hands off of her. She's now old enough to touch and the fire in his blood and the combination of pain killers make him lose control. Abby can't help but take what she's always wanted.

Together they have to overcome their fear of being left behind to grab what they have always wanted-each other.

A Saint's Salvation (the Santiago's book 1)

Corporal Nicholas 'Saint' Santiago needs to go home to reclaim the man he used to be. To be the man he was before Operation Enduring Freedom slowly hardened his heart. He needs to reconnect to the values and the reasons he is doing what he does. Saint also needs to try to forget the courageous woman he fell in love with.

Petty Officer Angelina Jones' life changed the moment Saint saved her life. She survived the blast but now has to deal with the fact that she will never be whole. She can't believe that anyone would want her the way she is now. Digging up her courage, Angelina moves forward hoping against hope that she can live a full life again.

Crossing paths again brings their emotions to a full boil. A coincidence that will have them both reaching for their dreams.

A Sailor's Delight (the Santiago's book 2)

Lee Santiago went from one mistake to the next. When a friend dies, exposing his mortality all too well Lee's family steps in to force him to make something of himself. He can't be a party boy all his life and if he wants to sign his life away, it will be on the dotted line. He doesn't even have time to say goodbye. Anyway it was only a drunken one night stand.

Isabelle was always the good girl. Until that night. When the man she'd always worshiped finally noticed her. She couldn't say no. She's heartsick to find out he doesn't remember it. Isabelle's life crashes around her when the results are in. The truth comes out and she has nowhere to turn. She looks for Lee, but he's gone.

Will he be man enough to step up and face the consequences when he learns the truth?

www.ingramcontent.com/pod-product-compliance
Lightning Source LLC
Chambersburg PA
CBHW061312170626
46817CB00001B/148